THE TEXAS TATTLER

All the news that's barely fit to print!

Fortune Fiancée Arrested For Murder

A media frenzy erupted last week when a blood-red ruby bracelet found at the scene of a heinous crime led police to the doorstep of the Double Crown Ranch. A seemingly stunned Lily Cassidy, Ryan Fortune's fiancée, was taken into custody and awaits trial for the murder of Sophia Fortune, Ryan's *wife*.

The megamogul has been in a grueling divorce standoff with second wife Sophia, who refused to bow out of their marriage even though hubby's offer would have made her a millionaire—many times over. Ever-devoted Ryan has been keeping constant vigil at the prison and swears on his Texas-sized integrity that Lily is innocent. Still, the district attorney continues to mount a strong case, making Lily out as the sort of woman who'd stop at nothing to get her man...

and his money.

And in the wake of this shocker comes the next...the life of Victoria Fortune, international do-gooder, is reportedly at risk. Sources confirm that the knockout nightingale became stranded in San Bonisto when the tiny, remote nation broke out in civil war late last month. Fearful father Ryan has commissioned mercenary-for-hire Quinn McCoy to smuggle the heiress back to safety. But those close to the fiery innocent know she doesn't kowtow to anyone, especially her father's errand boys—even when *this* "errand boy" is 100% virile man!

D0951757

About the Author

BEVERLY BARTON

Beverly Barton has been in love with romance since her grandfather gave her an illustrated edition of *Beauty and the Beast*. An avid reader since childhood, Beverly wrote her first book at the age of nine. She wrote short stories, poetry, plays and novels throughout high school and college.

After marriage to her own hero and the births of her daughter and son, Beverly chose to be a full-time homemaker, a.k.a. wife, mother, friend and volunteer. These days Beverly's children, who are the joy of her life, are adults, out of college and on their own. With the addition of a son-in-law and daughter-in-law, Beverly now has the four children she always wanted. She and her husband are absolute fools over their young grandson.

After over thirty years of marriage to the love of her life, Beverly is a true romantic and considers writing romances a real labor of love. Her stories come straight from the heart, and she hopes that everyone who reads them will feel all the strong and varied emotions she invests in her books. She truly believes that there is no power greater than the power of love.

The author of thirty novels, Beverly is a member of Romance Writers of America and helped found the Heart of Dixie chapter in Alabama. Since the release of her first Silhouette book in 1990, she has won the Georgia Romance Writers Maggie Award and the Laurel Wreath Award and is a two-time winner of the National Readers' Choice Award. Beverly is a RITA Award, a Holt Medallion and a Colorado Award of Excellence finalist and a *Romantic Times Magazine* Reviewer's Choice nominee. Her books consistently make the Waldenbooks bestseller list and often hit the *USA Today* bestseller list.

In the Arms of a Hero

BEVERLY BARTON

Silhouette Books

Published by Silhouette Books

America's Publisher of Contemporary Romance

Special thanks and acknowledgment are given to Beverly Barton for her contribution to The Fortunes of Texas series.

SILHOUETTE BOOKS

ISBN 0-373-65039-6

IN THE ARMS OF A HERO

Visit us at www.romance.net

Printed in U.S.A.

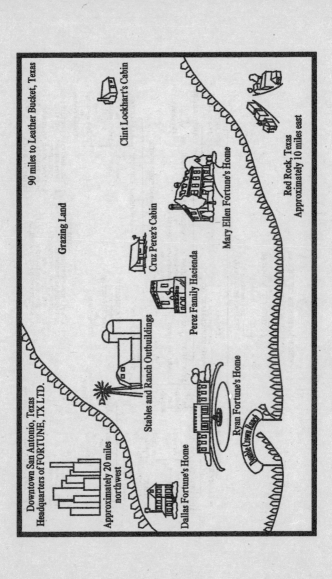

THE FORTUNES OF TEXAS
KINGSTON FORTUNE (d)

1st marriage
PATIENCE TALBOT (d)

Teddy §

2nd marriage
SELENA HOBBS (d)

MIRANDA
m Lloyd Carter (D)

KANE GABRIELLE ⑨
m
Wyatt
Grayhawk

RYAN

1st marriage
JANINE LOCKHART (d)

ZANE ⑫ DALLAS ④ VANESSA ② ****VICTORIA ⑩
m Devin Kincaid

MATTHEW
m
Claudia Beaumont

1st marriage m
Sara Andersen (d)
2nd marriage m
Maggie Perez

Bryan

2nd marriage
SOPHIA BARNES

CLINT LOCKHART
brother of
JACE LOCKHART ⑥
m
Ciara Wilde

† ROSITA and RUBEN PEREZ

Anita Carmen Frieda CRUZ ③
m
Savannah
Clark

MAGGIE ④

1st marriage
m
Craig Randall (D)

Travis

2nd marriage
m
Dallas Fortune

CAMERON (d)
m MARY ELLEN LOCKHART

HOLDEN ① LOGAN ⑤ EDEN ⑦
m
Lucinda
Brightwater

m
Sheikh
Ben
Ramir

Amanda
Sue*

Sawyer**

LILY
REDGROVE
m
Chester Cassidy (d)

m Emily
Applegate

COLE* ⑪ HANNAH ⑧ MARIA
m
Parker
Malone

James a.k.a.
Thaylor

* Child of affair
d Deceased
D Divorced
m Married
*** Twins
† Loyal ranch staff
§ Kidnapped by maternal grandfather

TITLES:
1. MILLION DOLLAR MARRIAGE
2. THE BABY PURSUIT
3. EXPECTING IN TEXAS
4. A WILLING WIFE
5. CORPORATE DADDY
6. SNOWBOUND CINDERELLA
7. THE SHEIKH'S SECRET SON
8. THE HEIRESS AND THE
   SHERIFF
9. LONE STAR WEDDING
10. IN THE ARMS OF A HERO
11. WEDLOCKED?!
12. HIRED BRIDE

THE FORTUNES OF TEXAS™

 Meet the Fortunes of Texas

Victoria Fortune: Her life was on the line, and out of nowhere hero Quinn McCoy arrived. And soon days spent dodging danger with the handsome stranger led to nights of passion. But was it just the moment or could it be forever kind of love?

Quinn McCoy: Protecting former debutante Victoria Fortune was turning into the mercenary's most perilous assignment ever...because this time he was in danger of losing not only his life, but also his heart.

Lily Cassidy: When Ryan Fortune's wife was found murdered, all fingers pointed to the billionaire's soon-to-be third bride. Did Lily resort to murder to clear her path down the aisle with Ryan?

Cole Cassidy: He couldn't stand idly by and let his mother go to jail. But would he be able to prove Lily's innocence before it was too late?

To my wonderful editor, Lynda Curnyn,
whose tireless efforts to help me make each book
the best it can be are greatly appreciated.

Prologue

"**I** can't guarantee the man that I can bring his daughter home safe and sound!" Quinn McCoy narrowed his piercing blue eyes into slits as he glared at the closed door to Ryan Fortune's study.

Sam Waterman scrutinized his old friend, someone he trusted implicitly, despite Quinn's mercenary background and mean-as-the-devil reputation. Women considered the man good-looking, in a rough and rugged way. They were attracted to him like bears to honey. And he was definitely a man other men respected and feared. Smart men. Those not so smart learned the hard way not to cross swords with Quinn McCoy.

As head of security for the Fortunes since Ryan Fortune, the patriarch of the family, had hired him, Sam took his responsibilities seriously. After the man's grandson had been abducted right out of his own crib, more bodyguards had been added to protect the family. It seemed unfair that with Ryan already having to deal with his fiancée being accused of murdering his former wife and his grandson being kidnapped that he now had to worry about his daughter Victoria's safety.

But Sam knew, without a doubt, that the hard-boiled gun-for-hire was a godsend for the Fortunes—the only man on earth he felt certain could bring Victoria home to her family.

"I told Ryan you were the best, that you're worth every penny of what he's offering you," Sam said. "Just go in there and talk to him. He's a father who's worried sick about his child. He'll give you anything you want, if you bring Victoria home to him."

"And what happens if I go after this spoiled little heiress and don't bring her back?" Quinn turned his speculative gaze on Sam. "Ryan Fortune is one of the most powerful men in the U.S. and not someone I'd want as an enemy."

"But if you succeed, he'd be your friend for life."

"Do you know how slim the odds are that I'd be able to make it in and out of Palmira, let alone bring Victoria Fortune out alive, now that Santo Bonisto is at war?"

"Just talk to Ryan before you make your decision." Sam rapped loudly on the closed door.

"Come in!"

Sam opened the door. Quinn hesitated.

Ryan Fortune rose from behind his massive desk, his dark eyes surveying the man Sam ushered into his private domain. Sam waited for several minutes, allowing the two men to size each other up and as-similate their gut reactions. As two bucks about to go into battle over a doe, the wealthy, powerful older man studied the lean, broad-shouldered warrior while the younger man defiantly met his perusal with a cool, confident observation of his own.

Before Sam could make the introductions, Ryan rounded the edge of the desk. "So you're Quinn McCoy."

Quinn didn't so much as flinch. "So you're Ryan Fortune."

The corners of Ryan's lips twitched as if he were going to smile, but instead he nodded to a manila file folder on his desk. "I know everything there is to know about you, Mr. McCoy, from your shoe size to how many fillings you have in your teeth. You've lived a rather dangerous, exciting life, haven't you?"

"Yeah, I suppose I have."

"Sam tells me that I can trust you, Mr. McCoy. His faith in you is the reason you're here today," Ryan said. "The reason I'm willing to offer you half a million dollars to bring my daughter back to Texas."

Quinn let out a long, low whistle. "I've been offered some fat fees before, but nothing close to five hundred thousand!"

"You don't have children, do you?" Ryan asked.

"No. Why?"

"If you did, you'd understand how I feel. My baby girl has gone and gotten herself caught right in the middle of a civil war in Santo Bonisto. She's in grave danger now, but if the rebel forces find out she's my daughter, they'll kidnap her and God knows what could happen to her. I want you to go in there and get her out of that hellhole before anything does happen.''

"I don't see why you ever let your daughter go to a Third World country like Santo Bonisto," Quinn said.

"If you knew my Victoria, you'd know that no one allows her to do anything. She's her own woman. And in her own way, as stubborn as her old man." Moisture glazed Ryan Fortune's brilliant dark eyes. "My girl has a big heart. Since she was just a kid all she's wanted to do was be a nurse, to ease other people's suffering. And now her idealism is putting her life at risk. When I talked to her this past week, she told me she couldn't desert the people in Palmira because she's the only trained medical help they've got. She's letting her loyalty and concern for those people make her act foolishly."

"I can't guarantee her safe return. Once I land on the island, anything could happen."

Sam had known Quinn long enough to realize by what he'd said that he was going to take the job. Had seeing, firsthand, a father's barely controlled agony actually swayed Quinn? Sam wondered. Or did he think of this assignment as simply another challenge? Few men were qualified for such a dangerous job and even fewer would have a snowball's chance in hell of actually bringing Victoria Fortune off that South American island powder keg. But Quinn McCoy had the credentials. A former navy pilot turned mercenary. A man who'd traveled the globe as a bodyguard, private pilot and all-around soldier of fortune.

"I understand," Ryan said. "All I ask is that you do everything within your power to bring my daughter safely home to us. I'm prepared to deposit a quarter of a million dollars into your bank account right now and another quarter million once you return with Victoria."

"And if I can't—"

"The quarter million is yours, if you come back alive, with or without Victoria."

"Fair enough."

"If there's anything else you need, all you have to do is tell Sam and he'll see that you have it." Ryan turned his gaze on Sam. "This family has been through enough. We *will not* lose anyone else we love."

"I understand," Sam assured Ryan.

"Mr. Fortune, there's one big item I need before I head off for Santo Bonisto," Quinn said.

"What's that?"

"My old plane is in pretty bad shape. I'd feel more confident about getting on and off the island if I—"

"Sam, get Mr. McCoy a new plane. Whatever he wants!"

Sam nodded agreement, then gave Quinn a deadly glare. He knew Quinn didn't have much use for the idle rich. His friend didn't make any secret of his disdain for most of his wealthy clients, but it riled

Sam to think Quinn was taking advantage of Ryan at a time such as this.

Ryan Fortune held out his hand. "Do we have a deal, Mr. McCoy?"

"We have a deal, Mr. Fortune."

As soon as the two men sealed their agreement with a handshake, Sam ushered Quinn out into the hallway.

"You're getting greedy, aren't you, asking for a new plane?" Sam gripped Quinn's shoulder.

"I'm risking my neck to even go into Santo Bonisto. There's a fifty/fifty chance I won't make it back alive. And you and I both know what will happen to Victoria Fortune if the rebels get hold of her, so the odds of me bringing the spoiled little princess back to the U.S. are slim to none. My odds are better with a decent plane. Besides, I figure the old man won't miss the money."

"Sometimes, you can be a heartless son of a bitch."

A quirky grin curved Quinn's lips. "You know me too well, old buddy."

"What do you mean, all lines of communication with the outside world have been severed?" Victoria Fortune demanded as she slammed down the dead telephone receiver. "Are you saying I can't even contact anyone in the capital city?"

"Sí, Señorita Victoria, that is what I am telling you," Ernesto Hernando said. "The rebel forces are headed this way and they are destroying all communication lines as they approach the city."

"Then there's no way to get word out of here? No way I can contact my family in the United States?"

"When your papa called last week and asked you to come home, you should have gone then." Ernesto gazed at Victoria, his huge brown eyes filled with concern. "Now you are trapped here with us and if it is discovered you are a wealthy American heiress, your life will be in grave danger. I wish I knew a way to get you to safety, to get you out of Palmira and to Gurabo."

She patted Ernesto's thin brown arm. "I can't leave you and Dolores here alone to cope with the clinic. As much help as you both are to me, neither of you has any medical training, other than what I've been able to teach you. And if the war does reach Palmira, I'll be needed here more than ever."

"You are an angel, *señorita.*"

Ernesto stared at Victoria with such admiration and devotion that she blushed. In the three years she'd been working through the World Health Institute, as the only nurse at the small clinic in Palmira, she had become close friends with Ernesto and his wife Dolores. During her first month at the clinic, Victoria delivered the couple's third child, little Rico Fortune Hernando. Named in her honor because she had saved the premature infant's life.

"We must make sure that everyone in Palmira knows not to reveal my true identity to any of the rebel soldiers," Victoria said. "I'm afraid with my red hair and green eyes, and my limited Spanish I'd never pass as a native. If necessary, I'll just have to use a false name and claim my papers were somehow lost or destroyed."

"*Sí*, the whole town will keep silent. You are greatly loved here. There is not one family who does not owe you their allegiance."

"From now on, I'll use the name Victoria Lockhart." She had instantly thought of using her mother's maiden name.

"*Sí, Señorita Lockhart.*" Smiling, Ernesto nodded agreement.

"We need to make preparations for the children's immunizations this afternoon. Sister Maria is expecting us at two o'clock."

Ernesto hesitated, but when Victoria smiled reassuringly, he turned to leave. Just as he reached the doorway, he paused momentarily and, without looking back, said, "We will find a way to keep you safe."

Before Victoria could reply, Ernesto slipped away quietly. She sighed. The thought that her presence here might put her friends' lives in danger unnerved her. She had to make Ernesto and Dolores understand that she didn't expect anyone to put their own lives on the line to protect her.

She had willingly chosen to come to Santo Bonisto, to live and work in the tragically poor little town of Palmira. Before she had set up a clinic here, the nearest medical facility had been a hundred miles away in Las Palomas. She had known the civil war would eventually reach her town, but she had hoped it wouldn't be this soon. Her father had demanded, in the way only Ryan Fortune could demand, that she return to the United States immediately. In attempting to make him understand why she couldn't leave, she had only made him angry. And she knew his anger was a result of fear. He loved her and wanted her safety above all else. She had promised him that she could stay in Palmira without endangering her life. But now she realized that there was every possibility she had lied to herself as well as her father. In her devotion to her duty, she had refused to admit the obvious. And now it was too late.

Just being an American in Santo Bonisto these days could be dangerous, if you were captured by the rebels. But if it was known that she was the daughter of one of the wealthiest men in the United States, nothing and no one could save her.

One

Quinn landed his new Cessna on an abandoned airstrip near a wide-open savanna halfway up Mt. Simona. Jungle surrounded the freshly cleared area. He could have demanded and gotten a more expensive plane from Ryan Fortune, but he had chosen a hundred-and-forty-thousand-dollar jewel. A larger plane would have had great difficulty landing, but the Skyhawk 172R breezed onto the narrow strip. The 172 didn't excel at anything in particular, not in style nor performance. But no other plane, on as little as 145 hp, could equal its overall performance. Quinn had chosen this particular plane for its dependability. In his chosen profession, that quality outweighed any other.

The airstrip built on the mountain plateau known as El Prado prior to World War II and left to the jungle in the early seventies had been forgotten by all but a few old-timers. Quinn never began an assignment without knowing the terrain of the country and searching out "associates" who could assist him. Julio Vargas, who waited for Quinn to disembark, had come highly recommended by "friends."

The short, stocky native, a machete in his hand,

greeted Quinn with a wide smile. "*Bienvenido!* Welcome to Santo Bonisto."

The sun kissed the mountain peaks above them, creating a colorful twilight. The sounds of oncoming night in the jungle resonated like distant music as a hushed stillness encompassed the secluded mountain plateau. A mad, high-pitched cry announced that a laughing falcon was nearby. The sound, so close to human hilarity, grated on Quinn's nerves. He scanned the area. A three-toed sloth hanging from a fig tree branch seemed to be staring at him. Ugly creature, he thought.

"Let's camouflage the plane and get out of here. I don't want to set up camp anywhere close by," Quinn said.

Coming in at night would have been ideal, except it would have required Julio to light the runway. Any unidentified light up so high in the mountains would have been suspect if seen by rebel soldiers. So coming in at dusk had been the wisest alternative. The plane, once hidden by brush, a lot of it removed from the runway itself, would be safe enough. As safe as any isolated spot on this godforsaken island.

He had done his homework on Victoria Fortune before flying out of Puerto Rico, after refueling there earlier in the day. The more he knew about the woman beforehand, the better his chances of persuading her to leave Santo Bonisto. The picture that had been included in the folder Sam had given him didn't look much like a sophisticated heiress. The fresh-faced redhead, with a splattering of freckles across her nose, looked more like the girl next door than a multi-millionaire's daughter. But her do-gooder complex marked her as lady who had more money than sense. Any woman in her right mind wouldn't be playing nursemaid to a bunch of peasants in a Third World country ready to blow sky-high at any moment. Just what was Ms. Fortune trying to prove? With her college degrees, she could be working in any hospital or clinic of her choice in the U.S. Or with her daddy's millions, she could be part of the jet-setting idle rich. So why had she become a member of the World Health Institute? And why had she stayed in Santo Bonisto when civil war broke out? Didn't she know that by staying in Palmira, she risked not only her life, but the lives of anyone who befriended her? And now she was risking his life—the sucker her father had hired to save her spoiled little butt.

"There is no time to set up camp, Señor McCoy." After laying aside his machete, Julio began dragging up brush to cover the plane. "You must go to Palmira as quickly as possible, if you wish to bring Señorita Fortune back with you."

Quinn lifted a heavy tree limb that lay on the ground. "What's happened?" He positioned the limb against the side of the plane.

"The rebel forces will be in Palmira no later than day after tomorrow. Perhaps as early as late tomorrow." Julio continued the process of hiding the plane from any aerial observance. "In order to reach

Palmira before daybreak, you must get started immediately."

"I thought I'd have more time."

"Your supplies are ready." Julio removed a rolled parchment from his jacket and handed it to Quinn. "The quickest and safest way to reach Palmira is to take a boat upriver. I have a boat waiting for you when you reach the Rio Blanco. Here's a map to guide you down the mountain and to the river. I have marked the exact location of the clinic in Palmira. I understand that Señorita Fortune has a room there."

"Just what will I run into on my way?" Quinn asked.

Julio disappeared inside the thicket to his right, then returned leading a heavily laden mule. He retrieved an M-16 and tossed it to Quinn. "Going in will be relatively safe. Coming out is another story altogether."

Julio grinned, exposing a wide expanse of rosy gum above a row of white teeth. He removed the backpack from the mule.

Quinn strapped on the pack, checked the M-16 and then opened the map. Scanning the map quickly, he noticed that Julio had outlined the rebel troop movements in the area. They were advancing toward Palmira at this very moment. If he didn't get in as soon as possible, he might not be able to find Victoria Fortune and get her to safety before all hell broke loose.

"I couldn't make any arrangements to aid you in

returning from Palmira,'' Julio told him. ''The rebel
forces have spies everywhere. Just a hint that someone from the outside was in the area would send off
alarm signals. If you need help while in Palmira,
contact Segundo. He works at the Cantina Caesar.
You can trust him.''

Quinn gripped Julio's shoulder and shook his
hand soundly. ''Keep an eye on my plane. If all goes
as planned, I should be back with my passenger before nightfall tomorrow.''

''If anything goes wrong, your best course of action is to head to Gurabo. There's a U.S. consulate
there, and for now, the capital city is still held by
the president's army.''

Getting Victoria Fortune out of Santo Bonisto
sounded as if it would be a simple operation. Travel
to Palmira, tell the woman her father had sent him
to fetch her home, bring her with him down the Rio
Blanco and up Mt. Simona, then fly her back to
Texas. An uncomplicated task—if rebel soldiers
didn't already have Palmira practically surrounded.
''My gut instincts tell me not to count on this being
easy.''

''Sí,'' Julio said. ''A man should always listen to
his gut instincts.''

Victoria studied the man's face—young, handsome, and deadly still. His big brown eyes stared
sightlessly up at the ceiling. She had lost him. Tears
clouded her vision. Emotion clogged her throat. She
had seen people die before, had attended elderly pa-

tients on their deathbeds and children passing away after suffering with incurable diseases. But this was her first experience with a soldier whose body was riddled with shrapnel. And he was only one of many who had been brought to the clinic from a battle less than twenty miles from Palmira. Nationalist soldiers were trying valiantly to protect Palmira from the horde of savage rebels blazing a path of death and destruction on their march toward Gurabo.

With gentle fingers she closed the youth's eyes, then lifted the sheet to cover his bloody body.

"Move this man onto the back porch," Victoria instructed Felipe, an elderly Palmira resident who had volunteered to help with the onslaught of wounded men being brought into the clinic. "There was nothing I could do for him. And I'm sure there will be others who will die tonight. Go to the church and bring Father Marco. He's needed here. Then see if you can round up some men to..." She took a deep, calming breath. "Someone will have to bury this man and any others who die."

"*Sí, señorita,*" Felipe said. "I go now." His weary, faded brown eyes gazed at her with the same adoration she often saw in Ernesto's eyes. "You care for the soldiers who are alive. Let me take care of the dead."

Victoria nodded, then brushed her damp bangs from her forehead. Nightfall had brought cooler temperatures, but the day's humidity lingered inside the stucco walls, creating a steam bath effect. The crowded clinic, filled beyond capacity, reeked with body odor, medicinal scents, fresh blood and the un-mistakable stench of death.

Rain was badly needed—to ease the humidity, clean the air and to stall the rebel forces' descent upon the town. Most of the roads leading in and out of Palmira were either dirt or sparsely graveled and filled with potholes. If it rained, perhaps the Nation-alist troops could hold off the attack on the town until reinforcements arrived.

Victoria left the dead man with Felipe as she rushed toward Dolores, who was trying unsuccess-fully to hold down a delirious soldier. Before she reached them, Ernesto restrained the man while Do-lores prepared a syringe.

Her eyes met Dolores's and they exchanged a si-lent message that assured Victoria she could move on to someone else. Although she had worked long hours on many occasions and had handled emergen-cies from time to time, nothing could have prepared her for the onslaught of wounded men who littered the clinic. Some she could help, others she couldn't. The most she could do for several was to ease their pain. Less than an hour earlier she had operated on a middle-aged man whose black eyes reminded her of her father's. A strong, broad-shouldered soldier, who now lay hovering between life and death.

She wasn't a doctor, and a doctor was what these men needed. But she was all they had—their only hope. The burden of that responsibility hung heavily on her shoulders. She was needed here, tonight, as she had never been needed before in her life. And she suspected that in the days and weeks ahead, she would be needed even more.

Perhaps she'd been foolish to stay in Palmira, putting her own life in danger. But how could she have lived with herself if she had abandoned these people when they needed her the most? Some of the young soldiers were boys from Palmira who had volunteered in recent days. Two she knew by name lay here in her clinic now, both wounded and suffering. She had removed a bullet from Carlos's shoulder. He would live. The other boy, Aluino, wouldn't survive until morning. His body had been ripped apart. He had been beyond saving when he'd been brought to the clinic.

The entire town worked together, friends and families with a common goal. By morning there wouldn't be a Palmira citizen not involved in the effort to bring in the wounded, care for them, bury the dead or even go to the front lines to fight with the government soldiers. And there was not one person, if the time came, who would not lay down his or her life to protect *Señorita Lockhart.* These people were like a second family to Victoria. And as her own family, they were loyal and supportive. And they needed her far more than the rich and powerful Fortunes ever would.

Victoria stepped outside, slumped onto the steps and leaned her head against the wall. She hadn't slept in twenty-four hours. She was bone-weary. Her stomach growled, reminding her that she hadn't had a bite to eat since breakfast yesterday. Glancing into the sky, she sighed when she saw dawn spreading across the horizon, illuminating the world with a soft crimson glow. A red sky at dawn often meant rain. As she rested alone on the steps, she prayed for rain. Soon. This morning. Torrents of rain that would cleanse the earth and hinder the rebel troop's movements.

The sound of a ragged Jeep coming up the street caught Victoria's attention. More wounded, she thought. Men were piled into the back of the Jeep, their bodies mutilated beyond repair. Dear God, how much longer could she endure this horror?

As she stood she speared her fingers through her short hair, combing the tousled strands. When the Jeep approached the clinic, she noticed a foreigner— *el extranjero*—riding in the front seat. The man wasn't from Santo Bonisto. Although his skin was dark, it was tinted by a deep suntan. His brown hair was cut short, only a bit longer than a crew cut. He wore rumpled khaki pants, mud-splattered boots and his short-sleeved khaki shirt was open enough to reveal a tuft of dark chest hair. He was big, broad-shouldered and had the look of a desperado.

The man jumped from the Jeep the moment the driver stopped. An M-16 draped across his shoulder. Within seconds he was issuing orders, organizing the men who rushed out of the clinic to carry the wounded inside. Victoria wondered who this man was and what he was doing in Palmira, helping the soldiers. Had the Santo Bonisto Nationalists hired mercenaries to aid them in their fight? Or was this man some U.S. government agent sent to assist? Everyone knew that the recent discovery of oil in this small island nation had made its welfare of prime interest to the U.S. It was the oil find that had instigated the current civil war.

"*Señorita*, where will we put these men?" Ernesto asked as he watched the helpers carrying the men inside to the crowded clinic hallway. "There are no more beds and the hall is covered with pallets."

"What about the basement?" Victoria suggested. "We'll move around whatever we can down there, light some lamps and then make pallets on the dirt floor for the less seriously wounded. We'll have to move some of the other patients out to make room for those who need immediate attention."

Dolores emerged from the clinic, wringing her hands. "How many this time?"

"There are six wounded men," the stranger said. "We left behind two that were dead."

Dolores glared at the big Anglo. "Who are you?" she asked in her heavily accented English.

"Quinn McCoy, ma'am." He responded to Dolores's question, but his gaze was riveted on Victoria.

"You're an American." Victoria had suspected as much, but the man's deep, throaty Southwestern drawl identified his nationality.

"So are you." He looked her square in the eye and smiled.

A shiver raced up Victoria's spine. She didn't like

his smile. It was too cocky, too self-assured. And the way his gaze moved over her, languidly, appraisingly, almost seductively, unnerved her.

"What are you doing with these men?" she asked as she motioned to Dolores to go inside, not wait for her. "Has the United States sent down some military help for the Nationalists?"

"I'm not with the U.S. government. I'm self-employed."

When he moved closer to her, she instinctively inched backward, taking a couple of steps up the stairs toward the clinic entrance. "Does that mean you're a mercenary?"

"Yeah, I suppose that could be one of my job descriptions."

She nodded, then turned and hurriedly raced up the stairs, leaving the stranger behind, escaping from the odd sensation his searching stare created in her stomach. There was something dangerously unnerving about the man.

Just as she entered the clinic, she heard her name called out from somewhere behind her. *Victoria.* The voice that spoke her name was deep and dark and decidedly American. She whipped around and came face-to-face with the stranger. Sucking in her breath, she eased backward and lost her balance. He reached out and grabbed her shoulders to steady her.

"How do you know my name?" Her heart drummed madly in her ears. Was this man really a mercenary hired by the Nationalists or was he working for the rebels? Did he know who she really was, that her father was Ryan Fortune? Was he here to kidnap her?

"Don't look so worried—" he lowered his voice to a whisper as he leaned over and placed his mouth near her ear "—Ms. Fortune."

She gasped, then tried to pull out of his captive hold. "Who are you?"

"Quinn McCoy, mercenary, pilot, bodyguard. At your service, ma'am."

Victoria clenched her teeth. She didn't like that decided twinkle in his eye, as if he were playing a game with her and enjoying himself immensely. "I don't know what you have in mind, Mr. McCoy, but I can assure you that all I have to do is scream and a dozen men will come to my aid immediately."

"By all means, don't scream." A barely concealed chuckle underlaid his words.

"Then let go of me!" The moment she renewed her struggle, he released her.

Ernesto came up beside Victoria, taking a stance as her protector. "Is something wrong, Señorita Lockhart?"

Before she could reply, Quinn McCoy said, "Using your mother's maiden name as a ruse? Not a bad idea. But not even a fake name will protect you for very long once the rebels take over Palmira."

"How—how did you know that Lockhart... Just who are you, Mr. McCoy, and what are you doing here in Santo Bonisto?"

"I've told you who I am. And as for what I'm

doing in Santo Bonisto...I was hired to come here to—''

"By whom?" Her heart lodged in her throat. She had the oddest notion that she knew who McCoy's employer was.

"Your father," he told her, locking his gaze with hers. "He sent me to get you out of the country and bring you home to Texas."

"My father! I should have known." Placing her hands on her hips, Victoria glowered at her rescuer. "You can leave right now—and without me. Go back to Texas and tell my father that I'm needed here."

"I'm afraid you don't understand," Quinn said. "What you want or don't want doesn't enter into this equation. You're leaving with me today, before the rebel troops take over Palmira."

"That's where you're wrong. I'm not going anywhere. These people have no doctor. I'm the only trained medical staff here at the clinic. Now, with the war raging so close and all these wounded men being brought in, I can't possibly leave."

"Look, princess—" when Quinn took a step toward her, Ernesto blocked his path "—we can do this the easy way or the hard way. It's up to you. But one way or the other, you're coming with me. Today!"

"Then it's going to be the hard way," she told him, peering at him from around Ernesto's shoulder.

"Damn," Quinn mumbled under his breath. "I was afraid of that."

Two

"I don't have time to deal with you, Mr. McCoy! There are men dying all around us. They're my top priority at the moment." Victoria Fortune spun around and rushed into the clinic.

"Wait just a—" Quinn said as he bounded up the steps.

But Victoria's protector, a thin, haggard young native, held up his hand, halting Quinn's ascent. "If the *señorita* doesn't wish to leave with you, then we will not allow you to take her."

"You realize that her life is in danger, don't you?" Quinn asked.

"*Sí, señor.* I know what could happen to her if it is discovered by the rebel forces that she is an American heiress. But remaining in Palmira or leaving here is her decision to make, not yours."

"It's nothing to me one way or the other." Quinn shrugged. "But it matters a whole hell of a lot to her father. He wants his little princess home all safe and sound. And he's paying me a small fortune to make that a reality."

"You cannot take her against her will. We will not allow it."

"If you care so damn much about her, then I'd think you'd want to help me get her off this island before—"

"We will make sure that her true identity isn't discovered. We will keep her safe."

"You can't assure her safety and you know it. The only way she'll be safe is if she leaves Santo Bonisto." Quinn grunted when he noted the determined look in the man's dark eyes. No way was this guy going to help him.

"Go away, *señor.* Go back to America and tell her father that she will not leave the people who so desperately need her."

A frontal attack wasn't working, Quinn thought. Time to change tactics. Use a more subtle approach. "Maybe I can help out around here. I know some basic first aid. I've treated knife and gunshot wounds. If I can't get Ms. Fort—Ms. Lockhart to leave right now, then I could stay for a while and do what I can to help her."

The man eyed Quinn suspiciously, then held out his hand. "I am Ernesto Hernando. Your help will be appreciated."

Quinn shook the man's hand. "Nice to meet you, Ernesto."

"Do not think that by working alongside Señorita Victoria, you can talk her into leaving us. Her mind is made up. You won't change it."

Quinn gripped Ernesto's scrawny shoulder. "I'm going to help you patch up the wounded best I can, for now. But the honest truth is that somehow

I plan to find a way to persuade Victoria to leave with me today.''

"I will be as equally honest with you, Señor Mc-Coy—if you try to take her against her will, we will be forced to kill you."

"Since we're being so damn honest, *Señor Hernando,* you need to know that if any of you get in my way, I'll be forced to retaliate."

Ernesto nodded solemnly. "I thought as much."

"Then we understand each other perfectly, don't we?"

"*Si.*"

Quinn knew what war and death looked like. Up close and personal. But it didn't matter how many times he had experienced the senseless waste, he still wasn't immune to the suffering. A part of him could understand why Victoria refused to abandon these people. He had watched her for hours now as she tirelessly tended to the wounded. Whatever else Victoria Fortune was, she was no spoiled, helpless rich girl playing at being a nurse.

The shapely, long-legged redhead was a tough-talking, hardworking professional totally unintimidated by the enormous task facing her. He hated to be the one to take her away from these people, but he'd been hired to do just that. A job was a job. He never let his personal feelings interfere with his assignments.

Quinn had one more card to play and if that didn't sway Victoria, he'd be forced to take drastic actions.

When Ernesto's wife Dolores insisted that Victoria take a break and eat something, Quinn took the opportunity to follow her into the small, makeshift office that doubled as her bedroom.

"We have enough food for you, too, Señor McCoy," Dolores told him as he entered the office.

"No, thanks. But a cup of coffee would be great."

"I'll be right back with your coffee," she said in Spanish. "I hope you like it black. We have no cream or sugar."

"Black is fine."

He had learned the Spanish language gradually over the years, finding it useful in his line of work to know how to speak more than just English. He was fluent in Spanish and French, knew enough German and Italian to get by, and had gained a smattering of various other languages.

Victoria slumped down in the tattered swivel chair at her desk. She leaned her head back against the plaster wall behind her and closed her eyes momentarily. After breathing a deep, heaving sigh, she opened her eyes and stared directly at Quinn.

"Thanks for your help," she said. "You make a pretty good medic. Dare I ask how you gained your knowledge?"

Quinn sat on the edge of her desk. "In my line of work a guy needs to know how to keep himself and his associates alive."

Quinn took a long, hard look at Ryan Fortune's daughter. Her tan pants and white shirt were filthy,

stained with a combination of blood, mud and unidentifiable substances. Her short-cropped red hair
was damp with perspiration. Her thick bangs clung
to her forehead. Without a smidgen of makeup, she
looked about eighteen instead of the twenty-five he
knew her to be. The sprinkling of freckles that dotted her nose and cheeks added to the wholesomeness
she projected.

Bone-weary, dirty and disheveled, Victoria Fortune shouldn't have appealed to him, but she did.
And for the life of him, he wasn't sure why. She
was cute, in a clean-cut tomboy sort of way, but
definitely not his type. He wasn't usually attracted
to the cute type or the filthy rich. Victoria was both.

He'd had a few *dalliances* with the debutante sort,
and had found most of those ladies a little cool for
his liking. He preferred the more earthy types, the
ones who knew how to give as well as take. Maybe
that's what appealed to him about Victoria. Despite
her heiress status, she was obviously a giver and not
a taker.

"What are you staring at?" When she frowned,
her small, perfect nose crinkled slightly.

"At you, princess."

Squaring her shoulders, she sat upright in the
chair and glared disapprovingly at him. "I appreciate all you've done here today, but if you think
hanging around helping out will change my mind
about leaving Palmira—"

"Here's your coffee." Dolores entered the office,
then handed Quinn a cracked mug filled with steam-

ing black liquid. She glanced at Quinn and then at
Victoria. "Stay in here and rest for a while, *señorita*.
We have things under control for the time being."
She left the office and closed the door behind her.

"I've got something for you." Quinn reached inside his shirt pocket, pulled out a letter and handed
it to Victoria.

"What's this?"

"A letter from your father."

She made no move to open the envelope, just sat
there for several minutes staring at it. "I'm not sure
I want to read this. My father can be a very persua-
sive man."

"Don't you think you owe him that much? The
man has already paid me a quarter of a million dollars to come after you. That tells me your safety is
worth more to him than anything."

"Of course, you're right. I have to read it." She
ripped open the envelope, removed the one-page
missive and unfolded the handwritten letter.

> My dearest Victoria,
> I know you do not want to leave Santo Bon-
> isto, that you feel you will be abandoning the
> people of Palmira when they need you the
> most. But you must know that your life is in
> danger from the rebel forces. Being an Amer-
> ican puts you at risk. Being my daughter is a
> death sentence.
> I have hired a man, Quinn McCoy, whom
> my security chief, Sam Waterman, assures me
> is the best there is at what he does. Please, go

with Mr. McCoy. Let him bring you safely home to me. To your family.

You may think we don't need you, but we do. Now more than ever. Lily's trial date has been set. I cannot believe that she was ever arrested for murder, not my sweet, gentle Lily. I try to hide my worry from her and from the family, but the situation doesn't look good. The media is having a heyday with the situation saying horrible things about my lover murdering my wife. If these vultures had known your stepmother the way we did, they wouldn't make her out to be the wronged wife.

Even Matthew and Claudia have put aside their differences in order to lend their united support. Your brother and sister-in-law have suffered greatly since their precious little Bryan was kidnapped and I pray that, despite everything, they can save their marriage.

After all that your family has endured during these past months, don't you think we have all suffered enough? I cannot bear the thought of losing you. Don't add to my torment. Come home where you belong. Home where you are needed.

I love you,
Daddy

Her father knew all the right buttons to push. He knew her weaknesses. More than anything, she wanted to be needed, to help those who suffered as her mother Janine had suffered during her long, agonized bout with cancer. Victoria had been a child—only twelve—when her mother had died, but she had vowed then and there that she would dedicate her life to alleviating the suffering of others. She hadn't been able to save her mother, but her mission in life was to save as many lives as possible.

Now her family was suffering—not physical pain, but a mental torment that seemed to be spreading like wildfire, affecting one person after another. The kidnapping of her nephew Bryan. The breakup of her brother Matthew's marriage. The death of her wicked stepmother Sophia. The arrest of Lily, the woman her father loved.

Her father was right. Her family did need her. Her father needed her. She should go home!

But how could she leave Palmira? She had made a commitment to these people. They were counting on her. If she left with Quinn McCoy, there would be no medically trained person at the clinic. People would surely die without her.

But if I stay here, I could very well end up dead, she reminded herself.

Quinn watched the play of emotions on Victoria's face and knew she was torn between doing what her father asked and fulfilling her duty to the people of Palmira. If she agreed to her father's request, it sure as hell would make his job a lot easier. He didn't like the idea of having to force the woman to go with him. But if kidnapping her was the only way to get the job done, then that's what he'd do.

"Do you know what the letter says?" Victoria asked.

"No," Quinn said. "Sam Waterman gave me the letter sealed. But I figure your father asked you to come home and told you that your family needed you right now."

"He wants me to go along nicely with you, to put my life and the needs of my family first." Victoria tossed the letter on the scarred, wobbly desk as she shoved back her chair. She stood, then began pacing back and forth in the 10' x 10' room.

"His request doesn't sound unreasonable to me." Quinn's gut instinct told him that she was in the process of talking herself out of leaving Palmira, despite her father's pleas. "You've got to know that by staying here, you're signing your own death warrant."

"Possibly," she agreed. "But if I leave with you today, how many people will die because I'm not here to save them? Is my life worth the lives of countless others?"

Quinn released a loud huff, then rubbed his forehead as he chuckled. Damn stupid do-gooder! Out to save the world! The woman had a martyr complex! She was willing to die for the people of Palmira. Noble sentiments. But did she really have any idea what the rebel troops might do to her? Before and after they collected a sizable ransom from her father. And Ryan Fortune would pay whatever they asked. But he'd never see his daughter alive again.

"Your life is priceless to your father," Quinn said.

"I wish I could do as my father asked, but...I can't."

"Is that it? You've made your decision? You're definitely not leaving with me today."

She nodded.

"What do I tell your father?"

"Tell him— No, don't tell him anything." Victoria sat, then opened a desk drawer and withdrew a pen and paper. "I'll write a letter to him and you can deliver it when you return to Texas."

"Your last will and testament?"

She cut her eyes in Quinn's direction, the look one of pure disdain. "Haven't you ever cared enough about anything or anyone to risk your life?"

"Nope, can't say that I have." He eased up off the desk. "I've risked my life more than once, but it wasn't for any ideal or for anyone I cared about. It was always for money. That's the only thing worth risking your life for."

"Money is meaningless without integrity and self-respect and genuine—"

"Spoken like a woman born with a silver spoon in her mouth." Quinn leaned over the desk, putting his face only inches from hers. "I grew up a poor, motherless kid in Houston. I just barely managed to stay on the right side of the law. I can relate to these Santo Bonisto peasants a lot better than you can, princess."

Her gaze locked with his. She clenched her teeth

tightly. Her cheeks flushed. Aha! His remarks had hit a nerve!

"What's the matter?" he asked. "Do you feel guilty that you and your family are so rich and these poor people don't have a pot to piss in? Do you really think sacrificing your life is going to change one damn thing for them?"

"You're heartless, aren't you, Mr. McCoy?"

"Got that right!" He withdrew from her. "Somebody mentioned a cantina not far from here. I need a good stiff drink. I'll be back in about an hour to pick up that letter you're going to write to your father."

"Don't bother. I'll have Ernesto bring the letter to you. I assume you're going to Cantina Caesar. It's the only one in town."

Quinn opened the door, then paused to look back at her. "See you around, princess."

"I don't think so."

"You never know."

Segundo laid his meaty hand on the bar, placing his palm up as his mouth curved into a toothless smile. The massively built owner of the Cantina Caesar reminded Quinn of a Sumo wrestler.

"To arrange passage for two on the *Evita*, the only boat going down the Rio Blanco this evening, costs more than I anticipated." Segundo sighed. "Now that the rebel troops are within striking distance of Palmira, any form of escape has doubled in price."

"I understand." Quinn retrieved the money from a pouch in his backpack, then counted it out on the bar. "Did you make the other arrangements?"

"*Sí*. That, too, will cost—"

"Twice as much." Quinn added the extra cash atop the other bills on the bar. "When Julio told me that I could rely on your assistance, he forgot to mention how expensive your services are."

"You know how it is, *señor*. A man such as myself must make a living as best he can."

Quinn grunted. "Yeah, sure." He knew Segundo's type. He'd dealt with men like him many times in the past. They could be trusted—for the right price. "What's the latest news on the rebel troops? Will I have enough time to put this plan into action and get out of Palmira before they take over?"

"Maybe," Segundo replied truthfully. "My sources say it's a matter of hours before Captain Esteban and his regiment arrive in our little town. The Nationalist soldiers have already retreated and are moving out of Palmira as we speak."

"You'd better take down that flag." Quinn nodded to the gold, red and green flag displayed over the bar.

"I'll replace it with a rebel flag the minute their troops enter the town. By then, you and your friend should be headed downriver."

"Let's just hope your man is convincing enough to persuade Señorita Victoria to leave the clinic. There's no way I can go there and get her, without having to kill a few of her protectors. And I'd rather not take that route.''

"Pablo will convince her," Segundo assured Quinn. "By the time you arrive at the warehouse, he should be on his way there with the *señorita.*''

"I'm surprised you found someone in Palmira who would betray Victoria. Everyone seems totally devoted to her."

"I convinced Pablo that by tricking the *señorita,* he will be saving her life. He does this not as a favor to me and not even for your money. He does it because he does not want to see the *señorita* raped and killed by the rebel soldiers.''

Quinn's stomach knotted painfully at the image Segundo's words created in his mind. From what he had found out about Captain Esteban's regiment, Quinn didn't doubt for a minute that they would rape Victoria, as they would any of the Palmira women they singled out to pleasure them. Only if and when the captain discovered Victoria's true identity would he send her to General Xavier to use as a hostage. The rebel forces as a whole were no more brutal or immoral than the Nationalists, except for Esteban's men, who were known for their inhuman treatment of captives. But General Xavier would no doubt use Victoria and any other Americans as examples of his hatred and disdain for the United States government. Even if Ryan Fortune paid the ransom money the general would undoubtedly request, Victoria would never leave Santo Bonisto alive.

Quinn knew he had to get her out of Palmira before nightfall—before Captain Esteban took over the town. He sure as hell hoped Segundo's plan worked. If it didn't, he'd have no choice but to storm the clinic and take Victoria, even if it meant disposing of her protectors.

Reaching into his shirt pocket, he removed the letter Ernesto had delivered more than two hours ago. Victoria's letter to her father. The one explaining why she couldn't abandon her duty, why she was willing to sacrifice her own life for the people of one little, godforsaken town whose residents were expendable to both the rebels and the Nationalists.

Rage ignited inside Quinn. He had known some stubborn females in his time, but Victoria Fortune took first prize. He tore the letter in two, then ripped it to shreds. He didn't give a damn what she wanted, he wasn't leaving this island without her. Whatever message she wanted to give her father, she could deliver in person. Just as soon as Quinn took her home to the Double Crown Ranch.

"Please, Pablo, calm down." Victoria clasped the man's trembling hands as he babbled incoherently. "I can't understand what you're saying."

In the distance, artillery fire echoed through the jungle that surrounded the little town. With each passing hour, the sounds of war drew closer and closer. She knew that, before nightfall, the rebel troops would invade Palmira.

"My sister-in-law's baby is trying to be born.

Now. But something is wrong," Pablo explained, his speech slower and plainer. "We tried to bring her into town, to the clinic, but we had to stop because her pain is so great. She has been in labor since early morning and my wife says the baby will not come. You must take the baby from her belly, *señorita*. It is the only way to save both mother and child."

Victoria rubbed the back of her neck. She wished she could divide herself into a dozen nurses, all capable of doing a doctor's job. She had lost seven patients since early morning and two more were at death's door. But there was nothing she could do for either man. If she went with Pablo, perhaps she could save two lives by performing a Caesarean section. Although she had never performed a C-section back in the U.S., she had, because of her specialty in obstetrics, assisted on several occasions. Since arriving in Palmira, she had done one successful C-section, so she felt reasonably confident that she could help Pablo's sister-in-law.

"I hate to leave the clinic." Victoria turned to Dolores. "I'm sure it's only a matter of time until more wounded soldiers are brought in."

"You go with Pablo and save the mother and her child," Dolores said. "Ernesto and I can handle things here for a while. If you are needed, I will send for you." She turned to Pablo and asked him where he had left his sister-in-law.

Pablo stuttered, obviously still quite nervous. "In the old...old warehouse at...at the end of town."

Victoria hesitated, but when Pablo squeezed her hands and pleaded with her, she relented. "I'll be back as soon as I can." She pulled her hands from Pablo's. "I need to get my medical bag."

"Bless you, *señorita*. Bless you." Pablo, tears streaming down his face, bowed several times. "You do not know how important this is to me. To save a life is a very good thing."

Fifteen minutes later Pablo led Victoria into a ramshackle building on the outskirts of town. The interior was dark and dank. The aroma of whiskey permeated the air. The moment the door closed behind her, Victoria's sense of self-preservation kicked in. Something wasn't right about this.

"Where's your sister-in-law, Pablo? Is she in a back room somewhere?"

"No, *señorita,* my sister-in-law is not here."

Victoria turned to leave, but found Pablo blocking the doorway. Her heart raced maddeningly. Her stomach churned with fear. Dear God, she had walked straight into a trap. But the question was, whose trap?

She couldn't believe Pablo had betrayed her. She had treated his mother's arthritis, had vaccinated his children from disease, had treated his wife when she'd severely burned her hand, and had even set Pablo's broken leg. She would have staked her life on Pablo's loyalty. How could she have been so wrong about a person?

A shudder raced over Victoria's nerve endings. "Why have you brought me here? I thought you and your family were my friends. I can't believe you lied to me."

"I am sorry for the lie, *señorita*. Please, forgive me." Fresh tears formed in the corners of Pablo's eyes. "I do this to save your life. You must leave Palmira before the rebels take over. I have already sent Mama and Alva and the children to Alva's brother in the mountains. They left two days ago. Now, Señorita Victoria, you must go home to America where you will be safe."

She heard a noise from behind her and knew before she turned around who was standing there. Somehow Pablo had been convinced that bringing her here was the right thing to do, that by luring her into Quinn McCoy's trap, he could save her life.

"Tell the man 'thank you,'" Quinn said. "By bringing you here, he's not only saving your life, but the lives of anyone who would have tried to keep me from taking you."

Victoria turned slowly, then faced Quinn, her eyes glowering with loathing. He had tricked poor Pablo! She turned to Pablo and smiled weakly. "I know you believe you did what was best for me. I'll be all right now. You must go and get away, out of Palmira and to your family as soon as possible."

"*Sí.* I and several other men who have sent their families away are joining them tonight." Pablo bowed to Victoria. "Go with God, *señorita.*"

Pablo opened the door, then scurried down the deserted street. The rumble of gunfire echoed in the stillness. Dark smoke billowed up into the sky, temporarily blocking out the late afternoon sunlight and turning the blue horizon a sooty gray.

Her first instinct was to run out into the street, to try to escape from her captor. But before she could act, Quinn slammed the door shut, then grabbed her arm.

She whirled around, her eyes flashing menacingly at him. "Get your hands off me!"

He released her instantly. "I've got passage for two booked on a boat leaving Palmira in less than an hour. We're going to be on that boat. You can either come along willingly or I can knock you out and carry you over my shoulder."

"You wouldn't dare! My father isn't paying you to abuse me!"

"Princess, the last thing I want to do is lay a hand on you, but if you put up a fight, then I'm going to have to get rough. I'm afraid I didn't bring along any knockout drops. Stupid me, I thought any woman in her right mind would want to be rescued. But I'm now convinced that you aren't in your right mind."

She crossed her arms over her chest in a defiant manner and titled her chin haughtily. "Just what did you mean when you said that Pablo saved the lives of anyone who would have tried to prevent your taking me?"

"I thought the comment was self-explanatory. If we hadn't figured out a way to lure you from the clinic, I'd have had no choice but to storm the place and take you out. Ernesto had told me that he and several others would kill me in order to protect you. That being the case, I'd have had no choice but to kill them first.''

Victoria gasped. ''You would have killed Ernesto? What kind of man are you? Does my father know he hired a killer?''

''Yes, to questions one and three. And as for what kind of man I am—I'm a professional who gets the job done. That's why your father hired me. Why he's paying me the big bucks. A nice guy, I'm not. But then, a nice guy couldn't get you home to Daddy all safe and sound.''

''And you can?''

''I'm sure as hell going to try, even if I have to fight you, half this town and all of Captain Esteban's regiment. I've got five hundred thousand dollars waiting for me when I get back to Texas.''

''I thought you said it was a quarter of a million.''

''Half before I left and half when I return.''

Victoria stuck out her chin. ''Well, you'd better go ahead and knock me out because I'm not going to cooperate. If I thought you had a heart, I'd plead with you to allow me to return to the clinic. But since I know what an unfeeling, uncaring jerk you are, then just go ahead and—''

Her grabbed her so quickly that his actions surprised her. She cried out in protest, which prompted him to cover her mouth with his hand. She tried unsuccessfully to maneuver her teeth so that she could bite him.

''I'm beginning to think I should have asked your

father for more money.'' Quinn had no intention of knocking her out. He'd thought just the threat would be enough to bring her into line. With any other woman that tactic would have worked. But not with Victoria Fortune.

So what are you going to do now? a small voice chided. *How are you going to get her out of Palmira and down to the river without someone realizing you've kidnapped their guardian angel?*

He didn't have any time to waste trying to figure out a way to make her come around to his way of thinking. She already thought he was a ruthless killer, capable of just about any brutal act, so why not use her beliefs against her?

She struggled with him, trying to free herself from his hold and loosen his hand over her mouth. He jerked her forward, pressing her into his body. He felt the lushness of her breasts, which were hidden beneath the billowy white blouse she wore. She fit against him as if she'd been made to be in his arms. His sex throbbed at the intimate contact.

"You're going to walk out of here with me and act like you want to go. We're going to board that fishing boat docked at the pier and I'm taking you down the Rio Blanco. If you don't cooperate, I'll be forced to kill whoever tries to come to your rescue. Do I make myself clear?"

Her big green eyes grew wide and round. She nodded her head affirmatively.

"I'll remove my hand, but if you try to scream, I'll muzzle you."

He lifted his hand. She opened her mouth and took in a deep breath. They stared at each other for a moment before Quinn eased her away from him. He reached over and lifted his M-16, draped it across his shoulder and then checked the straps on his backpack.

Swinging open the door, Quinn grabbed Victoria's arm and pulled her out into the street. The sun lay low in the western sky, like a ball of melting orange sherbet. Victoria realized that she had to do whatever this man told her to do. At least for the time being. She didn't doubt for one minute that he was capable of killing anyone who got in his way.

With his big hand gripping her arm, Quinn led and she followed. Just as they exited the outskirts of town and headed down the dirt road leading to the river, a thunderous explosion rocked the earth beneath their feet. Crying out in shock, Victoria threw herself into Quinn's arms. He wrapped her protectively in his embrace.

"That was too damn close," he said. "Looks like Esteban's boys have arrived in Palmira. Let's get the hell out of here."

She ran as fast as she could to keep up with Quinn's quick pace, but after a few minutes, she felt as if he were dragging her. When she protested, he slowed his gait just enough to accommodate her. The river lay ahead of them, about a hundred yards. A rusty old boat that had seen better days sat anchored at the pier. The name printed on the side of the hull was barely legible, but Victoria thought it read *Evita*. A scruffy, breaded man wearing battered slacks and a dirty T-shirt stood on the deck of the boat. He looked as if he were waiting for someone.

He's waiting for us, she thought. Waiting to take them down the Rio Blanco, away from Palmira, away from the people who depended on her. What would Ernesto and Dolores do when they realized she wasn't coming back? How would they cope with the sick, the wounded, the dying?

Quinn threw up his hand and waved at the captain of the *Evita*. The man grinned, exposing two gold front teeth. He waved and motioned for them to come aboard. When they reached the edge of the pier, Quinn hoisted Victoria onto the deck, then jumped on board.

"We must hurry," the captain said in Spanish. "I want to be downriver before—"

A bullet whizzed past the captain's shoulder and pierced the metal bucket hanging on the pole to his right. Within seconds a squad of soldiers sprung out of the woods and descended on the pier.

"Get this tugboat moving," Quinn hollered to the captain as he shoved Victoria flat on her face to the deck. "Stay down!"

She lay flat on her belly, but lifted her head enough to see what was going on around her. Fear ate away at her stomach like a powerful acid.

A barrage of gunfire pelted the boat. A shot hit a crewman, who yelled as he dropped overboard into the river. Crawling across the deck several feet, Quinn eased his M-16 over the edge and aimed it at the oncoming soldiers. With the ease and precision of a highly trained mercenary, he mowed down the soldiers before any of them could board the boat. But within minutes another contingent of rebels emerged from the woods—twice as many men, with twice as many guns. If the captain didn't get the boat moving immediately, not even Quinn McCoy could hold off that many attackers.

Three

Victoria's body shook uncontrollably as she crawled across the deck toward Quinn. A barrage of bullets pierced the deck of the *Evita*, killing another crewman and wounding a third. The captain weighed anchor just as two soldiers leaped aboard the boat. Quinn rolled over quickly and aimed his M-16 at the invaders. Before either man had time to attack, Quinn shot each where he stood. Victoria covered her mouth to stifle a cry. Quinn glared at her, his piercing blue eyes issuing her a warning.

The rebel troops stormed the pier. Victoria's heartbeat accelerated so fast she felt as if she'd faint. But she'd never fainted in her life and wasn't going to let today be the first time. She crawled to Quinn's side, somehow feeling safer close to him. The thought wasn't a rational one. She acted purely on instinct.

Quinn's big body dripped with perspiration as he held their attackers at bay. He was like a one-man army, but Victoria wondered how much longer even he could hold off so many soldiers.

The boat's old single-engine motor groaned once, then a second time and a third, finally dying on the fourth try. Three rebels headed straight for the boat. Quinn shot one, but the other two managed to climb aboard.

The boat's engine groaned again. Victoria said a silent prayer. Suddenly the motor roared to life. *Thank you, God!* Now, maybe they had a chance.

The two soldiers separated, flanking Quinn. Victoria held her breath. What could she do to help him?

Quinn reacted swiftly, using the butt of the M-16 to smash into one rebel's head as he swung his leg high into the air in some sort of karate movement. His foot made contact with the other soldier's chest, tossing him backward onto the deck.

Just as the downed rebel started to rise, there was the sound of a gunshot and a bullet ripped through his body. Victoria glanced up at the helm and saw that the captain held a revolver in his hand.

The *Evita* eased slowly from the pier. Quinn reloaded his weapon. Running along the riverbanks, the soldiers continued firing at them. Before he took aim again, he glanced over at Victoria.

"Keep your head down, princess. We're about to make our getaway."

She nodded agreement, but didn't think he saw her. His attention focused on the task at hand. She slumped over and closed her eyes.

So this is what war is truly like, she thought. No amount of television coverage could depict the harsh reality of soldiers killing and being killed. How could anyone endure it? Brutally taking another's life to stay alive.

In his years as a mercenary, how many men had Quinn McCoy killed? Didn't it bother him at all to annihilate so many men in one battle? Apparently he was more than just an ordinary expert at this sort of thing. No doubt about it, her father had gotten his money's worth when he'd hired Quinn.

But she had no right to condemn Quinn. Not when he had just saved her life. However, if he'd left her in Palmira, she wouldn't have been caught in the cross fire. She would be safe at her clinic. But for how long? She had no way of knowing for sure what the rebel troops would have done to her. Even now, Captain Esteban's troops could be murdering every wounded man at the clinic.

She should be there, with Ernesto and Dolores. She was needed... The soldiers would rip through the town and then leave it in ruins. Afterward, her services would be needed even more than now. If she could find a way to escape and return to Palmira, she could hide out until the rebels moved on, then go to the clinic. There were people who would help her, if only she could get away from Quinn.

Once the boat cleared the riverbank, leaving the rebels behind, Quinn draped his M-16 over his shoulder, then inspected the bodies lying on deck. One by one, he hoisted the corpses and dumped them overboard. Victoria watched in silent horror as he disposed of the men he'd killed. She found herself repulsed by Quinn and yet at the same time strangely drawn to him, too.

She didn't like her father's hired gun, in fact she almost hated him. But after recent events, she had gained a grudging respect for his expertise. Obviously, Quinn was a man accustomed to getting things done, regardless of what it took to accomplish his objective. He was, most definitely, a man you'd want on your side in any battle.

What would such a man be capable of doing to protect a woman he cared for, a woman who meant something to him?

"Looks like you've got work to do," Quinn said.

"What?" Still stunned by her oddly romantic thoughts, it took Victoria a couple of seconds to realize he was referring to the two wounded crew members. "We left my medical bag at the warehouse, so I don't have any supplies with me, but I'll do what I can."

"I'll help you see to them."

He followed her to the starboard side of the creaking vessel, where both men lay on the deck.

"Shouldn't you keep watch or something?" she asked. "What if the rebel soldiers are following us?"

"My guess is that Esteban's men are too busy burning, looting and ravaging Palmira to worry about following us. Besides, I don't think there are any other boats in Palmira, especially none that could make the nine, ten knots the *Evita* probably can. And as far as I know, General Xavier doesn't have a navy at his disposal.''

Victoria cringed at Quinn's comment about Palmira being ravaged at this very moment. Thoughts of her friends' safety came instantly to mind. ''I should be at the clinic with Ernesto and Dolores.''

''What's your problem, princess? Do you have some sort of death wish?''

Quinn bent to one knee and lifted the bloody crewman's limp body, then turned him over very slowly. The man groaned in pain. The exit wound had created a large gaping hole in his stomach. Shutting her eyes momentarily, Victoria admitted to herself that there was nothing she could do for this man. If she had some morphine, she could make his dying easier. But she had no medical supplies of any kind.

''Do you suppose the captain has any medicine?'' she asked Quinn.

''I doubt it, but my bet is he has plenty of whiskey aboard.'' Quinn made direct eye contact with the crewman, then spoke to him in Spanish. ''Take it easy. We'll do what we can for you.''

''Go ask the captain if he has any whiskey,'' Victoria said. ''I'll check on the other crewman and see how bad a shape he's in.''

Quinn nodded, then headed toward the cockpit, from where the captain steered the *Evita* down the Rio Blanco, slowly but surely taking them farther and farther away from Palmira. She watched the captain making hand motions when Quinn approached him, but she was too far away to hear what was being said. Suddenly remembering there was another man in need of her medical attention, she hurried over to check the crewman lying a few feet away.

The young man forced himself up on his elbows. His mahogany face turned ashen. Victoria inspected him visually, from head to toe, and found the bullet hole in his pant leg.

"I don't think it's bad, *señorita*." he told her. "But it hurts very much."

While she ripped the pants up to his thigh, she heard whispers and mumblings. Glancing over her shoulder she noticed several people coming from below deck, and realized, for the first time, that she and Quinn weren't the only passengers aboard the *Evita*. She didn't recognize anyone, so she doubted they were from Palmira. Had these people come downriver hoping to escape the forward-moving band of rebel soldiers? Three men, one woman and two young children emerged cautiously, their attention caught first by the wounded crewmen and second by the redheaded Anglo.

Victoria examined the man's leg. "The bullet will have to be removed. Otherwise gangrene could set in and you'll lose your leg."

"Ask your man to take the bullet out," he said. "Please, *señorita*."

"What's your name?" she asked.

"Chico."

"Hello, Chico. My name is Victoria—"

"Here's the whiskey!" Quinn shouted.

Victoria gave him a puzzled look. Why had he yelled at her? She wasn't deaf. "Thanks. Now, if you'll take care of—"

Quinn grabbed her arm, then jerked her to her feet and up against him. He hissed his words into her ear. "Don't tell anyone your name!" He glanced around and saw that the other passengers were watching them. "Hi, there, Chico," Quinn said. "I'm Quinn McCoy and this is my wife, Victoria."

Quinn's deadly glare warned her not to contradict him. He was right, of course, she realized. They had no way of knowing who they could trust.

"Chico has a bullet in his leg that's going to have to come out," she explained. "He wanted you to—"

"Fine. I can handle it. Here, you take this whiskey—" he shoved the bottle into her hand "—and go do what you can for that man over there." He nodded toward the dying crewman.

"But I should be the one to take care of Chico's leg. After all I am a nur—"

"You're my wife," Quinn reiterated. "You'll do what I tell you to do. You see to the dying and let me remove the bullet from Chico's leg."

Her cheeks crimson, her eyes narrowed to angry slits, Victoria stomped across the deck. After sitting, she lifted the dying man's head onto her lap. She opened the cap and placed the whiskey bottle to his lips.

After only a few sips the man stiffened, then went limp. Victoria checked his pulse. He was dead. She gently closed his eyes, then eased his head onto the deck.

"Do you need any help?" she called to Quinn.

He looked up from his examination of Chico's wound. "Bring the whiskey with you," was all he said.

"Is Franco dead?" Chico asked.

"Yes, I'm afraid he is," Victoria told him as she handed Quinn the whiskey bottle.

Victoria leaned against the railing, letting the night breeze cool her face and body. A full moon illuminated the murky water beneath them and the dense jungle that surrounded them. Vine-covered trees lined the banks of the winding Rio Blanco. Cascades of greenery swayed gently, their silhouettes dark and foreboding.

A pair of screeching macaws, their long tails drooping behind them, flew from one bank to the other. An ant shrike cried out from the jungle.

"Time to go to our cabin." Quinn slipped her hand into his. "We both need some sleep before the captain puts us ashore near Delicias early in the morning."

"How early?" she asked.

"Probably around two-thirty or three," he said. "We go from Delicias up Mt. Simona to El Prado, where my plane is waiting for us."

"If all goes as planned, you should have me back in Texas by tomorrow night, shouldn't you?" She fought the urge to jerk her hand free of his, but knew that if she hoped to escape, it was best to cooperate with her kidnapper.

"If all goes as planned." He tugged on her hand. "Come on. After the day we've had, we could both use some rest."

She allowed him to lead her down the stairs, below deck and straight to the smallest of the three tiny cabins. Inside the closet-size room, stacked bunks hugged one wall, leaving an open space of only a few feet on the other side.

"Sorry that there's no facilities in the cabin for a bath," Quinn said.

"I can take a bath when I get home to the Double Crown."

"Your old man's ranch is really something," Quinn said. "It's like a small kingdom."

She smiled coyly. Being friendly with Quinn should set him at ease, perhaps convince him that she had finally accepted defeat and wouldn't give him any more trouble. She wanted him off guard. He needed to relax just enough to allow her to leave the cabin without his being aware that she was gone. She would have to wait until he was asleep, then she would speak privately with the captain. If she could persuade him to set her ashore at the nearest village, surely she could find someone willing to help her get back to Palmira.

"Is that why you call me princess, because my father's ranch is like a kingdom unto itself?"

"Yeah, something like that." He surveyed her from head to toe. "You take the top bunk."

She forced herself to continue smiling, although she realized he wanted her in the top bunk because it would be more difficult for her to crawl down and get out the door without his hearing her. All right, so getting away from him later would be more difficult. So be it. She could be as quiet as a mouse if necessary. When he awoke several hours from now, he'd have no idea she wasn't still asleep in the bunk above him.

"Sure thing." She lifted her foot to place it on the first rung of the wooden ladder.

"Need any help?"

Before she could reply, he placed the open palm of his big hand flat against her buttock, then gave her a shove. She gasped at the intimate contact. Hurriedly, she scooted into the bunk and laid her head on the rumpled pillow. Her rear end tingled where Quinn had touched her. Get over it, she told herself. Quinn was the first man who'd ever touched her that way who didn't think of her as either a kid sister or just one of the boys. Quinn's touch, no matter how innocent, had possessed a sensual quality. At first contact, it had seemed as if her were caressing her.

Now, why would Quinn McCoy be attracted to you? a little voice asked. *You're hardly the type who drives men wild with passion. All your life, you've been a tomboy and none of the guys you've been around ever treated you like a woman.*

Then she remembered. *The man likes money. And my father has millions. He told me himself that money is the only thing that's ever mattered to him.*

Quinn sat on the edge of the bunk. His back and shoulders ached. He had the beginnings of a rotten headache. But he didn't dare fall sound asleep. If he knew Ms. Fortune, and he believed he did, she would make a run for it, straight to the captain, the minute she thought he was asleep.

Why couldn't the fool woman get it through her head that Palmira—actually anywhere on Santo Bonisto—was the last place on earth she needed to be?

He could tie her to the bunk, he supposed, but a part of him actually liked the idea of chasing her down and bringing her back to the cabin. What he really wanted to do was to give her a good spanking. He figured that was what was wrong with her now. She'd probably grown up without the least bit of discipline. Rich parents usually let their kids get away with murder.

Victoria might have outsmarted the men in her life up to now. Or perhaps she had used feminine persuasion to get what she wanted. But not this time. There was no way he was going to allow her to return to Palmira. She might be willing to risk her life to fulfill her promises to the locals, but he wasn't willing to let her take that risk. The only promise he'd made was to Ryan Fortune. A promise that he'd do his best to bring Victoria home to Texas.

Quinn stretched out on the bunk. His feet dangled off the end. His shoulders were broader than the bunk, so he turned sideways to make room. Every muscle in his body screamed. He was tired, sleepy, and sore from head to toe. He longed for a good night's rest.

If he feigned sleep too soon, she was bound to become suspicious and probably wouldn't make her move. He had no choice but to bide his time before he allowed her to slip out of the cabin and make a mad dash straight to the captain. Even if for some reason he didn't catch her before she cornered Captain Martinez, her pleas would fall on deaf ears. When he'd borrowed the whiskey earlier that evening, he'd made arrangements with the captain. Money talked. And at present, despite Ms. Fortune's wealth, she didn't have a dime to her name. But Quinn did. And wasn't it ironic that the money belonged to daddy?

Quinn grinned. He was actually looking forward to chasing Victoria and subduing her. She was sure to put up a fight, since she had to know this would be her last chance to escape. By morning they'd be on their way to the U.S. He had seen glimpses of the hellcat inside Victoria, and just the thought of her spitting and clawing at him aroused him. He couldn't help but wonder how it would feel to make her purr.

Minutes ticked by. Quinn shuffled around in the bunk, letting her know he was having difficulty resting. She, on the other hand, didn't move, barely breathed. She's waiting, he thought. Waiting patiently for him to fall asleep.

After nearly and hour Quinn moaned, then quieted. Within minutes he was snoring loud enough to wake the dead. He lowered the volume of his snores, enough so he could hear her when she climbed out of the top bunk. He didn't have long to wait. Within five minutes she eased down onto the floor and hovered over him, checking to make sure he was really asleep. He continued the mock snoring until he heard the cabin door open and close.

Taking his time, he maneuvered his big frame out of the lower bunk, then stood and stretched. Should he allow her to make it all the way to Captain Martinez or should he cut her off at the pass? Either way, she was going to be fighting mad.

When he opened the cabin door, he found the narrow hallway empty. Only the old boat's creaking and the hum of the engine disturbed the eerie quiet. He climbed the steps to the deck and glanced toward the cockpit. There she was, halfway to the captain. After losing all but one of his crew—and that man was recovering from a bullet wound—Martinez had little choice but to pilot the boat himself tonight.

Quinn crept along behind her, waiting for the right moment to grab her. He wasn't sure what alerted her to his presence, but somehow she sensed he was behind her. She turned sharply. Her mouth opened on a silent cry.

"Going somewhere, princess?" he asked.

"I thought you were asleep!"

"I snore sometimes when I'm awake." Grinning, he took a step toward her.

She backed away from him. "You knew all along

that I'd make a break for it once you were asleep. You let me think I had a chance of escaping.''

"Call me devious." He moved closer to her. When she backed against the rail, he reached out for her.

She scooted down the railing, avoiding his touch. "I've got a few other choice words I'd like to call you."

When he reached for her again, she slapped at his hands. Just as she lifted her foot to kick him, she slipped. She lost her balance and fell backward over the railing. Her body hit the water with a resounding splash. Sputtering with fury, she screeched at Quinn.

"Don't just stand there," she told him. "Help me before the crocodiles eat me!"

"Hang on," he told her, then hailed the captain.

Quinn dove overboard, then swam over to her. When he pulled her to him, she didn't resist. The captain lowered a rope. He and two of the male passengers pulled first Victoria and then Quinn aboard the *Evita*. All the passengers, including the children, watched as the two soaking wet Americans were hauled onto deck.

"Sorry about all the fuss," Quinn said. "My wife and I were taking a moonlight stroll on deck and she just lost her balance."

The men all laughed and the women smiled demurely. The wide-eyed children seemed dazed by all the excitement.

Quinn clasped Victoria's upper arm and guided her down the steps and back to their cabin. After slamming the door shut, he locked it. She stood in the middle of the tiny room and glowered at him.

"Why couldn't you just let me go? I planned to hide out somewhere until the rebels left Palmira. I'd have found someone to help me, to hide me out until then."

"You're plum loco. Do you know that?"

"Isn't two hundred and fifty thousand dollars enough for you?" She pulled her shirt from under the waistband of her pants, then twisted the river water out of the material. "Do you have to have the entire half million? For once in your life, do something for the right reason, not for the money."

Quinn unbuttoned his shirt, removed it and hung it on the frame of the bunk bed. "You've got it wrong. If I make it back to the U.S. alive, your father pays me the other quarter million, whether I bring you back or not."

Victoria found herself gaping at Quinn's muscular chest. It wasn't as if she hadn't seen partially undressed men before. After all, she had a father and three brothers and cousins, and there had been ranch hands galore on the Double Crown. Not to mention all the men she'd treated as a nurse.

"You'll get the whole amount whether or not you return with me in tow?" She couldn't seem to move her gaze from his chest up to his face. "Then I don't understand what difference it makes to you."

Quinn removed his boots and socks, then unzipped his pants. Victoria's gaze moved downward.

Her eyes widened. Quinn tugged off his wet pants and hung them on the opposite side of the bunk bed.

"You might want to turn your head, unless you'd like to see everything," he told her.

She whirled around, turning her back to him. "You didn't answer my question. If you'll get your money with or without me, why won't you let me go?"

Quinn rummaged through his backpack, pulled out his one change of briefs, then slipped into them. The only other clothing he'd packed was a T-shirt, which he lifted up into his hand.

"You need to get out of those wet clothes."

"I'll be all right," she said stubbornly. No way was she going to strip with him right there in the room with her.

"All I've got dry is a clean T-shirt," he told her. "I'll leave it here on the bottom bunk, then I'll wait outside the door until you've changed. And I'd appreciate your hurrying. I wouldn't want to give any of the other women aboard this tugboat a thrill."

She stood stiffly, her back still to him as water dripped off her hair and clothing and puddled around her feet.

"If you're not changed when I come back through that door, I'll strip you myself!"

She spun around just in time to see him leave. She eyed the white T-shirt lying on the lower bunk. She had no choice but to follow his instructions, unless she wanted him to remove her clothes for her. The very thought of Quinn McCoy putting his hands on her sent shivers racing through Victoria's wet, chilled body.

As she hurriedly undressed, she caught herself eyeing the closed door, wondering how long Quinn would wait before returning to the cabin. She tossed the wet clothes on the floor, picked up the T-shirt and pulled it over her head. It was too large, of course. The hem struck her midthigh. But she didn't feel quite as naked as she'd thought she would.

He knocked on the door, then entered to find her stretched up on tiptoe to reach the frame of the top bunk, where she was hanging her shirt. Quinn took a good long look at her shapely legs. Allowing his gaze to travel upward, he noted the firmness of her behind barely hidden under his T-shirt. He liked what he saw.

Victoria turned to face him and gasped aloud when she realized that he wore nothing except a pair of cotton briefs that did very little to conceal. Forcing her gaze upward, she caught him staring at her breasts. She glanced down and noticed that her peaked nipples were clearly visible through the thin T-shirt. Instinctively she crossed her arms over her breasts.

Quinn closed and locked the cabin door, then took a couple of steps toward Victoria. "My T-shirt looks good on you. Mighty good."

"Don't you have anything else you can put on?" she asked him, trying desperately not to lower her gaze.

"Nope. I'm afraid not. I didn't pack for a vacation, you know. Does my state of undress bother you?''

''No, of course not. It's just that… Oh, nothing!''

Quinn removed a small vial from his backpack, unscrewed the lid and took a hefty swig of the liquor inside. ''Rot gut,'' he told her. ''My own particular brand.'' He held out the vial to her. ''Here, princess, drink a little of this.''

''I don't need—''

He shoved the vial in her face. ''Drink a little or I'll pour it down you. It'll calm your nerves, warm your belly and maybe help you rest a little.''

Hesitantly she accepted the silver vial, then lifted it to her lips and drank. She strangled on the strong liquor as it burned a path from her throat to her stomach. Quinn laughed when she coughed several times and held the vial out for him to take.

Her cheeks flushed pink. Her green eyes sparkled with a mist of tears. The dozens of tiny freckles that sprinkled her nose and upper cheeks seemed to have been hand painted with coppery gold dust.

Quinn shook his head to dislodge such fanciful notions. Where the hell had that thought come from? He never got sentimental over a woman. Any woman. Certainly not one he'd been hired to protect.

Quinn grabbed the vial, then shoved it into the backpack. ''Better turn in. It won't be long before we reach Delicias.''

She nodded agreement, then climbed up into the top bunk. Quinn stretched out in the lower bunk and wished the damn thing was longer and wider.

They lay there quietly for several minutes. He could hear her breathing and suspected she could hear him. He'd bet money neither of them would get any sleep. Something was going on between them—something he didn't like. He hadn't let a woman get to him on a personal level since he'd been a stupid kid, who thought with a particular part of his male anatomy instead of his brain.

"Quinn?"

"What?" He hadn't meant for his voice to sound so harsh.

"You never did answer my question."

"What question?" He turned sideways, trying to arrange a comfortable position for his aching body.

"Why are you determined to take me back to Texas, if my father's going to pay you the full half million even if you don't bring me back with you?"

"Let's just say that when I'm hired to do a job, I do it."

"Is that the only reason?" She stared up at the ceiling, her heartbeat erratic as she waited for his reply.

"What other reason could there be?" He socked his fist into the small, lumpy pillow beneath his head.

"I don't know. I thought maybe…"

"Maybe what?"

"Never mind."

"Don't go thinking it's anything personal," he said, trying to convince himself as much as her. "I wouldn't leave any woman to the likes of Esteban and his men. I've seen what animals like that can do to a woman. And it's not a pretty sight.''

"I understand.''

"No, you don't. And that's the problem. You have no idea.'' Quinn's body tensed at the thought of any man putting his hands on Victoria, of some rebel soldier brutalizing her. "But believe me, princess, as long as there's breath in my body, nobody's going to touch you.''

Except me.

Four

Quinn and Victoria arrived in Delicias before
dawn. The small village lay less than a mile from
the Rio Blanco. The bright moonlight illuminated
the narrow dirt path leading from the riverbank,
making their trek an easy one.

Quinn had rested, but hadn't slept during the
night. He suspected Victoria had done the same. She
hadn't protested or complained when he'd roused
her for their departure. He guessed that she wasn't
the type of woman who whined and griped about
her circumstances, a rarity for someone as wealthy
as she was. In his experience, he'd found that
spoiled rich girls were usually first-class bitches.

"Looks like the whole village is still asleep."
Victoria inspected the area, which was comprised of
about a dozen thatch-roofed dwellings. "Do you
have to contact someone here or are we simply passing through?"

"We're passing through," Quinn told her. "The
fewer people who know our whereabouts the better."

"Do you think you can find your way up the
mountain in the dark?"

"I found my way down in the dark. There's a pretty clear path all the way up to El Prado, so unless we run into something unexpected, we should make it to my plane well before noon."

As they bypassed the village, circling around behind the weather-beaten cottages, Quinn noticed a dim light shining through the windows of the last house they passed. Odd, he thought, that someone would be up so early. The farther they moved away from the village, the more that oddity bothered him. Over the years he had learned to listen to his gut instincts and right now they were telling him that something was wrong. Bad wrong.

He grabbed Victoria's arm to halt her. "We're going back to the village."

"What? Why?"

"I have a feeling something's not right. I want to check it out."

"What are you talking about?" She ran to keep up with him as he led her back to the village.

Breathless, she gulped in air when he stopped and pulled her into the shadowed corner of the last cottage. "Stay here and don't make a sound," he whispered.

"What's going on?"

"Lower your voice. And just do as I say," he told her. "There shouldn't be a light coming from that house. I'm going to check it out."

"You're awfully suspicious. Maybe somebody inside there is sick. Or it could be that the family is just getting an early start on the day."

"If that's the case, then fine, we'll be on our way. But I'm going to make sure. Now stay here!"

"Yes, sir!" She snapped the words on a whispered breath.

Quinn crept around the side of the cottage, easing up to the window. Keeping his body flat against the wall, he peered through the dirty, cracked glass pane. A metal coffeepot and a battered fry pan sat atop an old wooden stove in the left corner of the room. An unmade double bed hugged the opposite wall. A kerosene lamp burned brightly where it rested in the center of a rough-hewn wooden table. There, sleeping in a chair, his feet propped up on the table, sat Julio Vargas.

What the hell was Julio doing here? He was supposed to be up at El Prado guarding the plane! Quinn surveyed the one-room cottage, checking to make sure Julio was alone.

Quinn made his way back to Victoria, who stood as still as a statue. "Come on. It seems I was right. Something is wrong. Julio's in there—" he nodded to the cottage "—which means he's not where he's supposed to be."

"Where's he supposed to be?"

"Guarding my new Cessna, about a thousand feet up the mountain," Quinn said.

"Does this mean—"

"I don't know what it means." Quinn clutched her hand, then pulled her along with him as he headed for the cottage door. He placed her behind him, then tried the door. It opened instantly. "Stay behind me and keep quiet."

Quinn's silent footsteps carried him into the one-room cottage, without alerting its single occupant. As Quinn approached the sleeping man, Victoria held her breath. Using the butt of the M-16, Quinn knocked Julio's feet from the table. The man cried out, then jumped to his feet, taking a fighting stance.

"Señor McCoy!"

"What the hell are you doing here?" Quinn demanded.

"I knew you would probably return during the night," Julio spoke rapidly in Spanish. "I left the lamp burning, knowing you would understand that it was a signal for you to stop."

"Get to the point." Quinn glared furiously at Julio. "Why aren't you up at El Prado keeping an eye on my plane?"

"Oh, *señor,* I have very bad news for you."

Victoria's stomach plummeted. She knew that bad news for Quinn ultimately meant bad news for her.

"Spit it out!" Quinn was fast losing patience.

"The plane has been confiscated. While I was guarding your plane, rebel soldiers arrived on El Prado. I couldn't fight that many men, *señor.* I was barely able to escape with my life. If they had seen me, I would be dead."

"So, what did they do with my plane?"

"I do not know for sure, but I overheard them talking about it. They know now that an outsider flew into Santo Bonisto. This is very bad for you and the *señorita*. You cannot return to your airplane. There will be soldiers waiting there for you.''

"Damn!" Quinn knew he shouldn't be surprised. He'd figured all along that this little rescue operation would turn into a real nightmare. Without the plane, they had no easy escape off the island. And now that the rebel troops were aware of a stranger's presence on the island, they'd be looking for him. They'd assume only an enemy would land on Mt. Simona and hide the plane.

"What do we do now?" Victoria asked.

"Please, Señorita Fortune, sit down," Julio said. "Allow me to fix you something to eat. You must be hungry and tired after your escape from Palmira. Lucky for you that Señor McCoy rescued you when he did. Otherwise…" He made the sign of the cross and mumbled some sort of prayer.

"Go ahead and sit," Quinn told her, then turned to Julio. "Do you have any coffee?"

"*Sí.*"

"Put on a pot. We've got plans to make before we leave." Quinn pulled out a chair, shoved a startled Victoria down onto it and then hung his M-16 on a chair across the table from her and dropped his backpack to the floor. "We have no choice now, but to use my backup plan."

"I don't know what that plan involves," she said, "but since we apparently aren't flying out of here today, you could just take me back to Palmira. The rebel troops will probably move on in a day or two, then we could—"

"For the love of Mike, lady, give it a rest!" Quinn shook his head in disgust.

"No, *señorita!*" Julio cried. "You cannot return to Palmira! The rebel troops who found Señor Mc-Coy's plane were talking about you. They knew that 'the Fortune woman,' the rich American lady, was in Palmira. Someone in Palmira told them you had left the town and that you may have gone with the American stranger who showed up yesterday. They said that Captain Esteban had plans for you before he took you to General Xavier. I am sure when they find that you are no longer in Palmira, they will be searching for you."

"Great!" Quinn slumped down into a chair. "Now we've got rebel soldiers looking for both of us."

"You must get Señorita Fortune off of Santo Bonisto as soon as possible," Julio said. "I will do what I can to help."

"Get us that coffee. Then we'll discuss an alternate plan."

Victoria sat quietly, allowing her mind to assimilate the information. People often said she was headstrong, willful and determined. She supposed she was, supposed she always had been. She had wanted to stay in Palmira, and even now, she longed to return and help those who needed her. However, it was plain that she could not go back to Palmira. No one had ever called Victoria Fortune stupid. And she finally realized that staying on Santo Bonisto would be stupid. She had fooled herself, as well as

Ernesto and Dolores, into thinking she could keep her true identity a secret from the rebel army. But she couldn't continue lying to herself, pretending that she would somehow be immune to the violence around her.

She was smart enough to accept defeat when she knew the cause was hopeless. She'd done all she could do. She'd held on to the bitter end—until Quinn had kidnapped her. And now that the rebel army knew the nurse who had worked at the Palmira clinic was Victoria Fortune, she couldn't return. If she did, not only would she sign her own death warrant, but that of anyone who tried to protect her.

"What's your backup plan?" she asked.

"We'll have to go to Gurabo and arrange passage off this island with the U.S. consulate."

"How to you propose we get to Gurabo? The capital city is on the other side of the island. Some of the roads leading there have been taken over by the rebel forces."

"We won't take the main roads," Quinn said. "It'll take us longer to make the trip, but using the pig trails will be safer."

"And just what sort of transportation do you suggest we use?" Victoria asked snidely. "I didn't notice any cars or trucks or Jeeps in this village. As a matter of fact, I didn't even notice a corral with any horses."

Julio set three earthenware mugs on the table. "There are no horses in Delicias. And no vehicles of any kind."

Victoria gave Quinn a see-I-told-you-so look. "Wonder how long it will take us to *walk* to Gurabo?"

"No need to walk all the way," Julio said. "My cousin Fidel has a fine truck and for the right price, he will be happy to sell it to you."

"Just where is Cousin Fidel's truck?" Quinn asked.

Julio lifted a dented metal pot from the woodstove, then brought it to the table and poured strong, hot coffee into the mugs.

"Fidel lives in Luquillo. It is perhaps a one-day journey on foot. I will provide some supplies for the trip. And I will show you, on your map, the safest way to get there from here."

Victoria lifted the mug to her lips. The black coffee had a distinctively bitter taste, but it was warm and refreshing. No doubt the caffeine would help her stay awake and at least partially alert. The last thing Quinn needed to deal with today was a woman asleep on her feet.

"Do you think we'll encounter any rebel troops between here and Luquillo?" she asked.

"I do not think so," Julio replied. "Unless General Xavier dilutes his forces by dividing them yet again and sending soldiers in every direction. There is no guarantee. Just because Luquillo doesn't lie in the rebel army's direct path, does not mean it will be spared."

"Do you have another gun?" When both Quinn and Julio stared at her as if she'd lost her mind, she explained, "In case we run into enemy soldiers, two guns would be better than one. Right?"

"What do you know about guns?" Quinn frowned, the gesture tightening his features.

"I was born and raised in Texas," she told him. "I grew up on a ranch. I've known how to use a rifle since I was a kid. And I'm a pretty good shot, if I do say so myself."

Quinn crossed his arms over his chest, leaned back in the chair and eyed her speculatively. "So if you had a weapon, you'd know how to use it?"

"Yes, I would."

"Got anything, Julio?" Quinn asked.

"Well, perhaps I have something the *señorita* can use." Julio lifted a plank in the wooden floor, revealing a hiding place. "Just a rifle. Nothing too fancy." He lifted an M-1 carbine, already loaded, then brought it across the room and handed it to Quinn. "I have others. A few handguns, too. Is this too much gun for the *señorita?*"

Before Quinn could reply, Victoria lifted the M-1 and inspected it. "I may need a little practice," she admitted. "But this one will be just fine for me."

"That's a lot of gun for—"

"For a spoiled, helpless heiress," she finished Quinn's sentence.

"She'll take it," he told Julio as he looked directly at Victoria. "I'll give you a few pointers on using the M-1, before we leave here. For now, let's eat a bite, look over the map and make our plans."

"All right. Whatever you say." Her steady gaze locked with his.

Quinn lifted his eyebrows as if doubting her sincerity. "Don't tell me that you've decided to stop fighting me every inch of the way. No more schemes to return to Palmira? No more heart-wrenching pleas to let you go back to the clinic where you're desperately needed?"

"Take a flying leap, McCoy!" He was the most infuriating man she'd ever met. He couldn't even begin to understand how she felt about her job with the World Health Institute or her devotion to the people of Palmira.

"Touchy on the subject?" He grinned at her.

Victoria wanted to slap that smug look off his face, but instead she controlled her rage. "From now until we get away from Santo Bonisto, I'm going to cooperate with you one hundred percent. But once we get off this island, I never want to see you again as long as I live."

"You've got yourself a deal." Quinn held out his hand across the table. "I can't wait to turn you over to your daddy and get rid of you."

Victoria placed her hand in his. He clasped it securely. They glared at each other as they shook hands, the emotional tension between them like a live wire. A strange tightness formed in the pit of her stomach. Fragile little quivers zinged along her nerve endings. What was wrong with her? Why was she reacting this way just because Quinn still held on to her hand?

There it was again, Quinn thought, that urge to take her over his knee and spank her. Or better yet, wrap his hands around her shoulders and shake her until her teeth rattled. Victoria Fortune irritated the holy hell out of him. And for the life of him, he couldn't figure out exactly why he reacted so strongly to her willful attitude.

"We must hurry," Julio said. "I will prepare you something to eat, then you must gather up your things and leave before the villagers wake. It is better for them and for you, if they don't see you."

The path Quinn and Julio had plotted on the map followed the course of the Rio Blanco for about five miles. When dawn spread across the eastern horizon, they crossed a rickety wooden bridge that spanned a deep gorge. Looking down the twenty feet below, they could see the water rippling over a shallow area dotted with dry-topped boulders. A small blue heron took flight and then landed farther down stream. Once across the gully, Quinn adjusted his backpack, then turned and checked hers. Julio had given them enough provisions to last three days.

"Only a precaution," he'd said. "In case something happens and you don't make it to Luquillo or if when you get there, you find that Fidel's truck is broken down."

The path turned toward the woods, winding along the outskirts of the dark, dense, verdant jungle. The narrow roadway they traveled led them farther from civilization. In spots the undergrowth had spread, trying to reclaim the cleared land. On those occasions, Quinn whipped out the machete Julio had provided and adeptly reopened the impassable road.

Only halfway up in the sky, the sun beat down on them unmercifully. Sweat trickled along Victoria's spine, dotted her forehead and pooled beneath her breasts. After traveling what seemed like days to her, but in actuality was less than three hours, Quinn suggested they rest. She knew that he had realized she needed a break, even if he didn't. On top of a ridge, they settled at a lovely spot where corozo palms speared their fronds toward heaven, creating a sun-dappled canopy. Victoria removed the floppy hat Julio had given her, then fanned herself with it as she slumped onto the ground.

Quinn handed her a canteen, which she opened immediately. The water tasted better than the most expensive champagne. She couldn't remember when she'd been this thirsty.

Quinn took the canteen from her, downed a couple of swigs, then returned the canteen to his backpack. "How tired are you?" he asked.

Worn to a frazzle, she wanted to say, but didn't. "Not too tired."

"You're lying, princess."

"What makes you think—"

"You're not a good liar. It shows on your face. So from now on you might as well be totally honest with me." He sat, crossed his legs beneath him and took out the map of Santo Bonisto. "If we don't take too many breaks, we'll reach Luquillo before nightfall. Then once we buy Fidel's truck, it shouldn't take us more than four hours to reach the U.S. Consolate in Gurabo.''

"Then let's not take any more breaks than necessary." Victoria shoved her floppy hat down onto her head. "I'm ready to go whenever you are."

He tapped the face of his wristwatch. "We'll stop every three hours and rest for thirty minutes. We'll eat lunch around noon and if we're lucky we can eat again tonight when we reach Luquillo. I've noticed you're in a better mood after you've been fed."

"Wish I could say the same about you, but food doesn't seem to help your disposition at all."

"Getting Fidel's truck will improve my disposition."

"It'll be wonderful to be able to ride the rest of the way to Gurabo," she admitted. "The heat and humidity really saps my strength."

"Why don't you lie back and relax," Quinn said. "Use your knapsack as a pillow."

"Good idea."

He helped her remove the small backpack. She spread out on the cool grass and closed her eyes.

"Want a snack?" he asked.

"What?" She opened her eyes and gazed quizzically up at him.

He picked up a corozo palm nut from the ground, then created a chopping block out of a tree root. With two precise machete chops, he removed one end of the nut and then the other. He handled the big knife with an expertise that implied great familiarity with its use. One final cut severed the nut in two, then he shared it with her.

Before she took the first bite, Quinn grabbed her and her backpack off the ground. Practically dragging her, he forced her into a thicket several yards from the palm trees. When she opened her mouth to speak, he pressed his index finger against her lips, silencing her. With his arm around her waist, he eased them both down until they were on their knees. She had no idea what was wrong, but his actions frightened her. Quinn wasn't a man who acted irrationally.

The jungle hummed all around them. A low, steady heartbeat of insect and animal activity. But over nature's melody came a louder sound—men's voices!

Her gaze met Quinn's. They exchanged a look of understanding. Who are they? she wanted to ask. We aren't near a village, are we? But she kept quiet, waiting, as Quinn waited, for people to materialize along the trail.

Within minutes a ragtag group of soldiers, armed with rifles and machetes, came into view as they cleared the rise. Seven men, ranging in age from teenage boys to one fellow well into his forties, wore dirty, sweat-stained, tattered uniforms. The emblem of the Santo Bonisto Freedom Fighters was emblazoned on their hats and across their shirtsleeves. Rebel troops!

Quinn gripped her hand, his strength reassuring.

She held tightly to him, her breath caught in her throat. What if they saw where Quinn had cut the tree roots to form the chopping block? What if they noticed the split corozo palm nut she had dropped when Quinn rushed her into hiding?

The soldiers didn't slow their pace as they passed the palm trees and headed in the direction from which she and Quinn had come. Were they on their way to Delicias? For the sake of Julio and the other villagers, she hoped not.

Quinn didn't allow her to stir for at least fifteen minutes after the soldiers disappeared. When he felt reasonably certain that it was safe for them to emerge from hiding, he helped her to stand.

"You stay right here," he told her.

"Quinn," she called after him when he left her.

"I'll be right back."

He inspected the path for several yards in both directions, but didn't detect any other soldiers. Maybe they'd gotten lucky this time and those seven rebels had been sent alone for some reason.

He could have mowed down the seven men and they never would have known what hit them. But then he would have had to dispose of seven corpses. Besides, he figured Victoria had seen enough bloodshed yesterday during their escape from Palmira to do her for a lifetime. He suspected she'd see a lot more before they escaped from Santo Bonisto, but he intended to spare her as much as possible. As long as it didn't endanger their lives.

"Come on out," he told her. "I believe the coast is clear."

"Do you think the rebels came from Luquillo?"

"Possibly. But there's no way to know for sure. However, I think the wisest thing for us to do is get off this road. If there are more troops in the area, they're bound to use it."

"How are we going to get to Luquillo?"

"The longest way around," he told her. "It'll take us a few more hours, since we'll have to make our own path through the jungle."

"Oh, great! The jungle! How much longer will it take?"

"We won't get to Luquillo tonight, which means camping somewhere and heading out again early in the morning."

"The way our luck is running, Fidel's truck will either have four flat tires that can't be patched or the gasoline tank will be empty, with no gas available."

Quinn forced himself to grin. No need to alarm Victoria unnecessarily. But they could face a bigger problem than having to do without Fidel's truck. If those seven rebel soldiers had come from Luquillo, there was a good chance that more soldiers had remained behind. And there was no way to be certain without going to Luquillo, or at least close enough to Fidel's village to find out what the situation was.

If the rebel troops were already in Luquillo, that lowered his chances of taking Victoria safely to Gurabo. And if he couldn't get her to the capital city, they were in trouble. Really big trouble.

"Quinn, what's wrong?" She clasped his arm. "What are you not telling me?"

Looking her square in the eye, he said, "I've told you everything you need to know right now."

Her first reaction was to protest his macho protectiveness, but on second thought, she decided to keep quiet. Even if she disagreed with him, she had to admit that in this situation, he was the expert, not her. If they were going to get out of Santo Bonisto alive, it came down to one simple truth—only Quinn's knowledge and ability could save them. Thank God, when her father hired a man to do a job, he always hired the best.

"All right," she said. "But promise me that if..." She hesitated momentarily, her gaze pleading. "If things become hopeless, you'll tell me."

"I promise." He skimmed her cheek with the back of his rough hand. The look in his eyes affirmed the vow he'd just made to her.

Long before nightfall, Quinn began searching for a place to make camp. Any place would suit Victoria. Any place she could lay her weary head. She was hot, dirty and tired. Every muscle in her body ached. The M-1 had grown heavier with every mile and occasionally she'd been tempted to dispose of it. And to make matters worse, the insect repellent Quinn had insisted she use possessed a distinctively repugnant odor that lingered on her skin.

They had been walking since dawn and if it hadn't been for the regular breaks Quinn insisted on taking, she wasn't sure she'd still be standing. They had been steadily climbing higher and higher and the altitude played havoc with her breathing. Quinn, on the other hand, seemed unaffected, which she knew wasn't possible. The man was, after all, human. Or was he?

During the trek through the jungle, Quinn had taken advantage of native pathways, but when there were none, he'd sliced his way through the thicket. Thankfully, the only problem they'd had to deal with, other than a couple of snakes, after their narrow escape from being caught by rebel soldiers had been Victoria's exhaustion.

"Up ahead," Quinn told her. "See that rock formation, the one that looks like a giant boulder?"

"Yes, I see it."

A variety of epiphytic plants encrusted the rough-surfaced boulder. The trees grew taller in this part of the jungle and the verdant canopy was thicker, blocking out the evening sunlight. An abundance of lush plant life sprouted from the moist ground. Compared to the sweltering heat of the tropical sun, the ravine seemed deliciously cool.

"We'll set up camp here," he said as he led her toward the sheltered spot beneath the giant boulder. "I can hear running water, so I'm pretty sure there's a stream nearby. I'll check it out later."

She sighed at the thought of burying herself in a

pool of refreshing water. "I'd give anything for a bath."

"Anything?" he teased.

She glared at him, but when she saw the lopsided grin on his face, her stinging retort died on her lips. "Well, almost anything," she corrected and returned his smile.

Quinn helped her remove her backpack, then removed his. When she started to sit on a nearby log, he clutched her arm to keep her from sitting.

"Let's put something over that log first," he said. "No use tempting any biting insects." He retrieved a rain jacket from his pack and spread it out for her.

Victoria's hips melted onto the jacket, then she bent, braced her elbows on her upper thighs and supported her head between her open palms. Quinn nudged her knee with the side of his calf. Lifting her head, she peered up at him. He handed her a canteen.

"Thanks." She drank her fill of the tepid water and handed the canteen back to Quinn.

"Rest here," he said. "But keep your rifle handy, just in case. I'm going to see if I can find that stream."

Don't leave me, she wanted to cry, but instead said, "I hope it's deep enough to swim in."

"If it is, we can go skinny-dipping."

Before she could respond, Quinn disappeared into the forest, leaving Victoria with her mouth agape. The thought of swimming in the nude appealed to her, but sharing that experience with Quinn McCoy ignited both apprehension as well as excitement within her.

Unfortunately the stream turned out to be narrow and shallow, providing no opportunity for a real bath. However, Quinn refilled their canteens from the underground spring that fed the small stream, which no doubt eventually spilled over into a larger stream that wound its way to the river. He stood guard, with his back to her, while she partially undressed and washed herself. Then she did the same for him.

They dined on tortillas Julio had packed that morning and on fresh fruit, washing it all down with cool water from the stream. Afterward, Quinn arranged two light blankets on the ground.

"Before you turn in, you'd better let me rub you down with insect repellent," he said. "You probably washed most of it off."

Victoria groaned. "I know I need that stuff, but I hate the smell."

Quinn chuckled. "It's not so bad. And with both of us stinking, it's kind of like eating onions and both of us having bad breath."

"Would you like me to do you first?" she asked, not realizing the suggestive connotation Quinn would give her words.

"Might be more fun if we *do* each other at the same time."

She stared questioningly at him for a couple of seconds, then realization dawned. "Oh, very funny,

Mr. McCoy. I was referring to applying the insect repellent, and you darn well know it.''

''Yeah, but a guy can hope, can't he?''

She didn't know whether to be flattered or offended. How could a woman know with a man such as Quinn? She assumed he was joking, hoping he could alleviate some of the tension their nerve-racking situation had created. But what if he'd been even partly serious? What if his teasing had actually been a proposition?

Get real, she told herself. *If Quinn wants me, it's because he needs a woman and I'm available.* Maybe he made a practice of seducing all the women he rescued. If that was the case, then she was definitely offended. She didn't like the idea of being lumped together with all the other women in his life— *Victoria Fortune, what are you thinking!* snapped that little voice. She was thinking about having sex with Quinn. A man she barely knew. A man she didn't especially like.

What was it about him that aroused such strong emotions in her?

Treat him the way you treat your brothers, the voice decreed. *Pretend he's just another of your male acquaintances who thinks of you as a buddy.*

No way on earth she could think of Quinn the way she did her brothers or her male friends. He was different from any man she'd ever known, and she was both attracted and repulsed by him in equal measures.

She rummaged in her knapsack for the insect repellent, making sure her eyes didn't meet his when she spoke. "If you're going to be offensive, then I withdraw my offer. You can just rub yourself—" She froze midsentence, realizing that once again he would twist her words to suit his own meaning. She grabbed the bottle out of the knapsack. "Oh, you know what I mean, so don't go getting all—"

Lightning-fast, he descended upon her, cutting off her breath as he snatched the bottle out of her hands and jerked her onto her feet. "Why don't you just stop talking while you're ahead, honey? If you keep this up, you're going to convince me that you're after my body."

Huffing loudly, her eyes wide and round, she shoved against his chest. "Of all the ridiculous things for you to... I'll have you know... Why, you're the last man on earth I'd—"

Quinn wrapped his arms around her, bringing her body intimately against his, aligning their lower bodies for a perfect fit. Gasping when she felt his blatant arousal, Victoria told herself to get away from him as quickly as possible. But her traitorous body refused to comply with her wishes. Instead she lifted her arms up and around his neck and gazed spellbound into his sexy blue eyes.

Five

I'm making a big mistake, Quinn told himself. Flirting with Victoria Fortune would be like playing with fire—he'd never know for sure who would get burned or how severely. But he couldn't help himself. How could he resist the look in her eyes, the feel of her breasts pressing against his chest, the seductive sensation of her arms wrapped around him? While his mind cautioned him to back off, to use common sense, his body responded as would any man's under similar circumstances.

Gripping her hip, he shoved her more intimately into contact with his hardened sex. Moaning deep in her throat, she closed her eyes. He lowered his head and touched her lips with a featherlight kiss. Her mouth opened on a tremulous sigh. Light shudders shook her from head to toe. With her lips parted, Quinn accepted the unspoken invitation to take what she was offering.

His kiss devoured. It ravaged. It possessed completely. He wanted her, wanted her badly. Here. Now. On the ground.

The overwhelming sense of belonging to Quinn erased any reservations Victoria had. In that one illogical moment, her mind ceased to function and she reacted purely on instinct. Something she seemed doomed to do again and again with Quinn.

Reserved at first, she returned his kiss shyly. But with each demanding thrust of his tongue, her self-restraint eroded until she claimed him as surely as he did her.

As a chained demon unleashed, Quinn's hunger controlled his actions; his mouth surveyed her face, her ears and her throat. All the while his hands explored her body, caressing, inflaming, heating his desire to the boiling point. When he covered her breast with one hand and squeezed, her closed eyelids flew open and she stared at him, the look a mixture of longing and surprise.

Victoria suddenly realized how out of control the situation had become and how easily she had succumbed to Quinn's amorous attack. He had swept her away with his passion.

Never breaking eye contact with him, she covered his hand with hers and removed it from her breast. Then she wriggled in an effort to free herself from his embrace. He released her slowly, as if doing so pained him. She stepped backward, putting several feet between them. He stood unmoving and silent. His breathing labored. His nostrils flared. His sex throbbed.

She didn't know what to say. Had no idea how to defuse the tension radiating between them. But she did know that if he touched her again, she'd be lost. Barely knowing Quinn and in spite of being uncertain about her feelings for him, she had to admit that she wanted him in a way she'd never wanted another man.

Quinn broke eye contact, turned on his heels and stomped away into the forest. Victoria slumped onto one of the blankets he had spread out on the ground. Why had she put her arms around his neck? Why had she allowed him to kiss her? Had she lost her mind? This wasn't some good-ole-boy friend of her brothers. He wasn't one of her college buddies. Nor was he one of her associates. He was a hired soldier of fortune, a ruthless stranger whose only interest in her was her father's millions.

Victoria curled up in a fetal ball, hugging her knees, as she listened for Quinn's footsteps. She waited and waited and waited. Her eyelids grew heavy. She yawned several times. Where was Quinn? Why didn't he come back and talk to her? Was he angry that she had rejected his advances?

Quinn watched Victoria from afar, knowing he had to stay away from her until he had regained complete control of himself. He didn't usually go off the deep end, the way he'd done with Victoria. It was as if she possessed some kind of unnatural power over him.

He'd had more than his share of women and sex had always been a wild ride for him. He kept his romantic liaisons on a strictly impersonal, sex-only, no-commitments basis. He liked things that way and sure as hell didn't want more from any woman. Certainly not from Victoria.

First of all, he was her bodyguard. Hired to rescue and protect her. He never became involved with clients, although he had been tempted a couple of times. Second, Victoria was out of his league. She'd been born with the proverbial silver spoon in her mouth, the daughter of a multi-millionaire. He always avoided personal entanglements with rich women. And third, he figured that Victoria wasn't the type to indulge in meaningless affairs. Even on such brief acquaintance, he suspected she was the kind of woman who'd confuse sex with love.

When he was certain she had fallen asleep, he returned to their makeshift camp. Gazing down at her in the moonlight, he couldn't help thinking about how young and wholesome she looked and how truly lovely she was. Trim without being skinny, slender without being delicate, her body was firm and toned.

The heat of day had died, leaving behind a damp coolness that seeped into the bones. After picking up his blanket, Quinn spread it over her. He positioned the M-16 at the edge of Victoria's blanket, then lay beside her and shared the cover. He turned his back on her, making sure their bodies didn't touch.

He didn't dare allow himself the luxury of falling deeply asleep so that he could truly rest. He doubted any rebel troops were moving through the jungle at night, but he wasn't willing to take any chances. His years of experience had taught him how to doze and yet remain alert enough to sense any hint of danger.

Victoria stirred in her sleep, uttering a tiny, gurgling sigh. Quinn's body tensed when she rolled toward him. Cuddling against his back, she threw her arm around his waist. He tried to shrug her off, but the harder he tried to dislodge her, the more she snuggled against him. Her full breasts pressed against his shoulder blades. Her thighs hugged the back of his.

He couldn't rest this way. Hell, if she remained glued to him this way for the rest of the night, he'd go stark, raving mad. Give it some time, he told himself. Sooner or later, she'd turn over and he would be able to move out of her reach.

So he waited as his body fought and lost the battle of control. This wasn't working, he admitted silently. She was draped all over him! He eased her arm from around his waist. She grumbled in her sleep. He sucked in a deep breath, hoping she wouldn't wake. Inch by inch, he slid away from her, untangling himself from the blankets. He maneuvered himself onto the damp earth, then turned in time to see her roll over onto her back.

Within minutes she began to snore. Quinn chuckled to himself. Poor kid, she had to be exhausted. After picking up his M-16, he reached down, lifted the edge of Victoria's blanket and covered her with it, tucking the edges around her. He took his own thin blanket with him as he headed toward the nearest tree. Using the blanket like a cape, he sat and braced his back against the knotted tree trunk. He laid his gun across his thighs, then closed his eyes and prayed for an uneventful night.

Quinn awakened Victoria at dawn, then hurried her through a quick breakfast of dried fruit and nuts. She seemed to be in a relatively good mood, cooperating with him fully. Neither of them mentioned what had happened between them the night before, but the fact was there, just below the surface, affecting everything they said or did. Both were now equally aware of the sexual tension that made each a little more wary of the other.

"If my calculations are correct, it shouldn't take more than two hours to reach Luquillo this morning," he told her. "We could be in Gurabo this afternoon."

"Let's just hope Fidel's truck is in working order."

"Think positive thoughts."

She pasted a halfhearted smile on her face as they headed off onto one of the many pig trails that dissected the jungle. She kept pace with Quinn, whom she knew had adjusted himself to her gait. During their trek, she found herself musing over the breadth of his shoulders, the slenderness of his waist, the tautness of his buttocks, the power in his arms and legs. No woman could deny that he was an incredibly beautiful male specimen. No, not beautiful, she thought. The word was too feminine to suit such a masculine man. Perfect was a better word. Perfect male specimen. Tall, but not too tall. Big, but not too big. Handsome, but not a pretty boy.

She wondered if he was thinking about her as she was him. Was he remembering the kiss they'd shared—the kiss that had almost gotten out of hand?

An hour later, moisture already coating her skin, Victoria longed for a drink of water. As warm and humid as the morning already was, she expected the day to be a real scorcher.

Quinn halted so abruptly that she ran straight into his back. He pivoted instantly, grabbed her by the arm and dragged her into the cover of the jungle. They dropped down on their haunches.

"What?" she asked, puzzled by his actions but at the same time realizing he had sensed some type of danger to which she was oblivious.

"Shh. There's someone out there," he whispered.

She listened. Heard nothing. They waited. After a few minutes she recognized the distant sounds—talking and crying. Not soldiers. Women and children!

"Quinn?"

"Yeah, honey, I know. Doesn't sound much like soldiers, does it?"

"Who do you think it is? We're not that close to Luquillo, are we?"

Quinn helped her to feet, then led her back onto the path. "Be prepared for anything. Have your gun ready, just in case. There's only one way to find out who they are."

Within minutes they encountered a group of natives, comprised of two old men and several weeping women and sniffling children. Quinn suspected, even before questioning them, that these people were from Luquillo, but an old man in his seventies, who seemed to be the leader, confirmed Quinn's suspicions.

"The rebels attacked our village early this morning," the old man, who had introduced himself as Alonzo Alverez, explained. "It was quickly decided that I and Manuel should get as many women and children out of the village as possible, but we—" he spread his arms "—are the only ones who escaped."

"What are the rebel troops doing in this area?" Quinn asked. "I thought General Xavier had the bulk of his army headed toward Gurabo."

"*Sí, señor*. This is true, but it seems Captain Esteban discovered that an American had landed a plane on El Prado and has disappeared. And the American nurse who runs the clinic in Palmira, also has disappeared. It is believed they are together. The soldiers were sent to Luquillo to search for them."

"What made the troops think this man and woman were in Luquillo?" Quinn asked.

Alonzo's weary gaze traveled from Quinn to Victoria, then returned to settle directly on Quinn. "Your friend and my nephew, Julio Vargas, was tortured until he told Captain Esteban that he had sent you and the *señorita* to Luquillo to buy his cousin Fidel's truck. Fidel is my grandson, *señor*, and he is now dead."

Victoria covered her mouth with her hand, silencing her gasp. Quinn glanced at her, then spoke to the old man. "The soldiers killed Fidel?"

"*Sí, señor.* To make an example of him. No one is to help the American man and woman. If they do, they, too, will be killed."

Victoria wanted to scream, *No! No, please tell me that we aren't responsible for the attack on Luquillo, for the murder of this poor old man's grandson!*

"Where are you and your people going?" Quinn asked. "Is there another village close by?"

She was amazed by Quinn's composure, by his lack of concern for what Alonzo and his people had suffered.

"Not close," Alonzo said. "But higher up in the mountains is a small village. My grandson's wife, Jacinta—" he pointed to a very pregnant young woman, who appeared to be in a trance and was being led by another woman "—was born in La Luz. Her family will welcome us, if we can make our way there."

"We'll do whatever we can to help you," Victoria said. "It's our fault that—"

"How far is La Luz?" Quinn interrupted her, knowing that if he didn't stop her, Victoria would promise these people the moon and stars—and then try her damnedest to deliver.

"La Luz lies on the eastern side of the mountain and is about four hours from here on foot," Alonzo said.

"Did any soldiers follow you when you left Luquillo?"

"No, *señor*. Once the soldiers took Fidel, I knew I had to act quickly. Manuel—" he glanced at the other elderly man "—and I didn't think two old men would be missed, so we hurriedly gathered Manuel's wife, two daughters and his grandchildren and my grandson's wife. Once out of the village, Jacinta turned to look back, hoping for a glimpse of Fidel. Unfortunately she saw the soldiers kill him."

"We're headed east, too," Quinn said. "It's only a matter of time before the men who attacked Luquillo come in that direction, to join forces with the other troops marching toward Gurabo. We don't have time to waste, if we intend to stay ahead of them."

Victoria grabbed Quinn's arm, then spoke to him in English, assuming none of the villagers would be able to understand her. "We must help these people get to La Luz. It's our fault that the rebels invaded their village and killed Alonzo's grandson."

Quinn glared at her as he jerked her up against him and said, "Stop blaming yourself. This country is at war and men like Captain Esteban don't need a reason to kill."

"Are you trying to tell me that you aren't going to help these people?"

"I'm saying my only objective is to get us to Gurabo and then off this island. I was hired to rescue you, not save a little group of displaced natives."

"How can you be so hard-hearted, so unfeeling?"

"Stop being such a damn bleeding heart!" He shoved her away from him so roughly that she nearly toppled to the ground.

When he reached out to grab her, she regained her balance and glowered at him. "I can't believe that, even for one minute, I thought you were...that you could be... I despise you, Quinn McCoy. Do you hear me? I think you're contemptible!"

"Think what you will," he told her. "But the truth is that no matter what we do, we can't change things for these people. Once this war reached them, they became a part of it, just as the people in Palmira did. You and I are only two people. And two people don't have much chance against a whole army."

"I realize that, but the least we could do is help these women and children get to La Luz. That's all I want to do. Tell me, is that too much to ask?"

Speaking in Spanish, Quinn issued an order to the two elderly men. "Show me—" he pulled the map from his shirt pocket "—where La Luz is located. If it's on our way to Gurabo, then we'll all travel together." Quinn patted the butt of his M-16, then glanced meaningfully at the M-1 draped over Victoria's shoulder.

Hurriedly, Alonzo pointed out the location. Quinn nodded his head and said, "Let's get moving." He took in the haggard expressions on the women's and children's faces, then his gaze lingered on Jacinta's swollen belly. "We'll stop as often as possible to let these people rest."

Victoria fell into step alongside Quinn, who led

them out of the forest and onto the well-worn path that skirted the Mt. Simona jungle. The path led upward, a gradual ascent that wound diagonally from the valleys and the Rio Blanco miles away.

"La Luz is on our way to Gurabo?" Victoria asked him in English.

Quinn neither slowed his pace nor glanced her way. "Yeah."

"You aren't worried about traveling the old roadway?"

"No."

"You don't think these people will slow us down?"

His jaw clenched. "I'm doing what you wanted, aren't I? So shut the hell up!"

Victoria stopped the smile before it touched her lips, but inside she laughed with joy. Quinn had an awfully loud bark and she didn't doubt for a minute that, when necessary, his bite was equally ferocious. But in this case, he'd been all bark and no bite. Was he doing this good deed for her sake? Or because he wasn't quite as heartless as he'd like her to believe? Whatever his motives, she was grateful. Leaving these poor people to fend for themselves would have broken her heart.

As they followed the uneven roadway, coconut palms and mango trees jabbed through the profusion of low shrubs and high grass along their path. After an hour they stopped to rest. She shared her water with the children first. Quinn held his canteen up to

Jacinta's lips. Victoria glanced at him and smiled.
He ignored her. Her smile broadened.

Halfway to their destination, they ran into trouble—the remains of a recent landslide blocked the
road. Quinn slashed a path around the rubble and
within fifteen minutes they resumed their trek on the
narrow pathway that had originally been created
ages ago by long-forgotten native tribes. The terrain
changed as they climbed ever upward and onward.
The low undergrowth that flanked them gave way
to towering pines. Overhead four black dots circled
in the sky. Turkey vultures. Victoria's stomach
tightened.

After two more breaks, their water gone and the
hot sun pouring down on them, she heard Jacinta
assuring the others that her parents' village was not
far off. Victoria looked to Quinn for confirmation.

"Another hour," he said. "How do you think
she's holding up?"

"Jacinta?"

"She shouldn't be making this trip in her condition, should she?"

"To be honest, I'm not sure she's feeling much
of anything," Victoria said. "I think the shock of
seeing her husband killed has dulled her senses. And
I'm not sure that's a bad thing, under the circumstances."

The closer they drew to La Luz, the steeper and
narrower the road, until finally it became only a path
that forced them to walk single file. Brush and
bracken covered the path in many places, their

heavy foliage like green arms reaching outward and upward to block the way.

Wiping away an errant strand of damp hair that had fallen across her forehead, Victoria glanced behind her to count their entourage. No one was missing. From her vantage point on a ridge above them, she saw that Alonzo and the other elderly man remained protectively at the end of the line.

When they stopped for what Quinn told them would be their last break before reaching La Luz, he asked who was thirsty. Victoria wondered why he'd bothered to ask since their canteens were empty and there didn't seem to be a stream anywhere nearby.

She stared in amazement when Quinn ripped a palm off a tree, a variety of bromeliad abundant in the tropics. A woman rushed forward with a jug she'd pulled from a cloth sack on her back. She removed a thin mesh scarf from the pocket of her skirt, then covered the lip of the jug with it. Victoria glanced inside the huge palm as Quinn tilted it over the jug. The brown fluid cupped by the palm, a reservoir for rainwater, turned her stomach. Flies, mosquitoes and other insects, along with unidentifiable decaying matter, floated in the liquid.

Once the woman strained the water, the villagers handed the jug from one person to another, but when they passed the jug to her, Victoria declined. She decided she wasn't thirsty, after all.

Quinn finished off the rainwater in the jug, then sat beside Victoria where she'd slumped on an enormous tree root protruding through the scraggly underbrush. He removed the map from his pocket, spreading it out for her to see.

"Here's La Luz." He pointed to the spot with his index finger, then traced a line eastward along the Rio Gurabo, to the capital city on the Atlantic coast. "And here's Gurabo. Once we reach La Luz, we'll eat, fill our canteens and rest for a while, but I want us on the road again while there's plenty of daylight."

"How far out of the way are we going by taking these people to Jacinta's village?"

"I wasn't exactly lying when I said La Luz was on our way to Gurabo." He grinned sheepishly. "We were heading east, anyway, just not higher up Mt. Simona's eastern ridge. We'll have to head down the mountain and follow the river to reach Gurabo."

Victoria laid her hand over Quinn's, which still held the map. Squeezing his hand tightly, she leaned over and kissed his cheek. "Thank you."

Without acknowledging the kiss, Quinn hastily folded the map, then returned it to his shirt pocket. He stood abruptly, turning his back to her as he walked over and began talking to Alonzo and Manuel.

Quinn McCoy was an enigma to her. A complicated man who was far more than he seemed to be. Every time she thought she had him figured out, he surprised her. But one thing she knew for sure, she no longer disliked him.

* * *

The residents of La Luz poured out of their thatch-roofed houses like bees swarming from a beehive. Others, who were outside, dropped whatever they were doing to stand and stare at the two Anglos leading the group of natives into the village. A tall, slender man threw up his arms and cried out, then rushed toward Jacinta.

"Padre!" Jacinta wept as he enclosed her in an embrace.

Alonzo greeted the man, calling him by name— Lucero.

Quinn led Victoria aside as the people of La Luz welcomed the villagers from Luquillo. Once introductions and explanations were finished, Jacinta's father, obviously some sort of village elder, shook hands with Quinn.

"Welcome to La Luz," Lucero said. "I am grateful that you have brought my daughter to me." He placed his hand on Quinn's shoulder. "Come, bring your woman and eat with my family."

Accepting the man's invitation, Quinn and Victoria followed Jacinta and Alonzo to the largest thatch-roofed shack in the small mountainside village. Jacinta's mother took her daughter into the smaller of the two bedrooms in the house, then returned to her guests.

After Jacinta's father prayed, giving thanks for the food and for his daughter's life, her mother served a simple meal of beans, rice and tortillas. Victoria savored every delicious bite, then downed a full glass of clean spring water.

"Alonzo tells me that you and your woman are on your way to Gurabo," Lucero said.

"Yes, we were hoping to reach the capital city today, but that was before... Well, we had thought we'd find transportation in Luquillo. Instead, we came across Alonzo and the villagers who had escaped."

"We will give you water and food for your journey down the mountain." Lucero motioned for his wife to refill Quinn's glass. "You are welcome to stay overnight."

"I'm afraid we need to leave as soon as possible," Quinn said.

"I understand. Alonzo says that your woman's life is in danger from Captain Esteban." Lucero inspected Victoria with a discerning eye, then nodded affirmatively, as if agreeing with himself on his decision. "A man would risk everything for such a woman when she is his."

Neither Quinn nor Victoria bothered to correct Alonzo's or Lucero's assumption that she was his woman. In their minds a man would risk his life for only one reason—for love.

Thirty minutes later, their backpacks in place and their rifles draped over their shoulders, Quinn and Victoria left La Luz.

"If we stay on the path, we'll make better time," Quinn told her. "I'm willing to risk it if you are. At least until we reach Rio Gurabo, then we'll follow the river. The quicker we can travel, the less likely the rebels are to overtake us."

"Whatever you think best." She smiled when she noted the look of surprise on his face. "What's wrong, shocked that I'm being so agreeable?"

"Yeah, but I know better than to think your amiable disposition is permanent. Sooner or later you'll return to your normal stubborn self and start refusing to take my suggestions."

"You don't suggest, Quinn, you order."

"Only when I know I'm right."

"Which you think is all the time," she said.

His facial expression sobered and he focused on her eyes. "If I give you any orders from here on out, take them. Obeying my orders could save both our lives."

She returned his serious stare, understanding only too well what he was trying to tell her. "I do know that now. Despite some of the things I've done, I'm really not stupid. Ever since you came to Santo Bonisto, you've been trying to save my life. I want to apologize for giving you such a difficult time when you first showed up at the clinic. I'd been lying to myself for weeks, thinking I could stay in Palmira and keep my true identity a secret."

He lifted his hand, as if to touch her, then let his hand fall to his side. "Tell me when you get tired. We need to keep moving as much as possible, but if you get so tired that I have to carry you, that will slow us down more than taking breaks."

"I'll let you know. I promise."

* * *

Less than an hour from La Luz, Quinn heard footsteps behind them. He took Victoria with him off the road, squatted and aimed his M-16. A skinny youth of no more than sixteen came into sight. A boy from the village. Quinn rose to his feet, then stepped onto the pathway.

"Señor! Señorita," the boy called out, breathless.

"What's wrong?" Quinn asked, fearing that the rebels had reached La Luz.

"Lucero says you must return to the village." The boy looked past Quinn to Victoria. "The old man, Alonzo, tells us that you are a nurse, *señorita*. You are much needed. Now!"

Quinn held up a hand to halt Victoria from running past him. "Who needs her?"

"Jacinta," the boy replied. "Her baby wants to be born, but Honoria, the midwife, says that the child will die. It is not time for the little one to be born. Not for many weeks."

"Then there's nothing the *señorita* can do," Quinn said.

She grabbed Quinn's arm. "But what if there is something I can do? In Jacinta's condition, she might die, too. I can at least try to save her and the child."

"This reminds me of Pablo's little fairy tale about his sister-in-law being in labor and needing you," Quinn said. "You're a sucker for pregnant women, aren't you, honey?"

"This is an entirely different situation and you know it! Jacinta really is in labor. And this time I actually might be able to save two lives. I'm a nurse, trained to—"

"If we go back to La Luz, we'll be putting ourselves in more danger than we're already in. Don't you see, you're doing it again? You're not thinking about saving your own life, so it's up to me to do it for you."

"Please, Quinn." She was not going to allow him to stop her. There was no way she could refuse to help Jacinta and then live with herself afterward, always wondering if the girl and her child had both died. "Leave me and go on to Gurabo, if you must, but don't force me to go with you. Two lives may depend on my returning to La Luz."

Quinn let out a long, loud huff, then cursed under his breath. "Dammit, woman, you're going to wind up getting us both killed!"

Bella Victoria Vargas came into the world at twilight, so tiny she could have fit in the palm of Quinn's big hand. She was perfectly formed, her head covered with soft, black fluff and her minute features already showing the promise of beauty. Her mewing cry reassured her mother that she was alive.

Jacinta had endured a painful labor process, but a relatively easy birth. The moment after she delivered the infant, Victoria laid the baby girl on her mother's tummy, then cut the cord and instantly wrapped the child in two small blankets that she had instructed

Jacinta's mother to warm in the oven of the wood-stove.

Alonzo and Lucero came into the bedroom while Victoria held the baby in her arms. Quinn stopped dead in the doorway. His gaze locked with Victoria's. Her closed-mouth smile spoke volumes. With that one smile, she thanked him profusely for allowing her to return to La Luz.

There was something about Victoria with a baby in her arms that affected Quinn oddly. Partly, he was in awe of her selfless devotion to the needs of others. And partly he was drawn to the maternal expression on her face as she cuddled the newborn before slowly positioning her in Jacinta's arms.

Victoria turned to the midwife and Jacinta's mother. "You both know that the baby must be kept warm. Heat rocks and wrap them and keep them in the bed with the baby."

Both women nodded their understanding, then Honoria led Victoria to a washstand. "You may clean yourself now, *señorita*. Then you and your man will stay at my house tonight. I will remain here with Jacinta and the child. If you are needed, I will send for you."

"Thank you. I've done all I can. The rest is up to God."

After Victoria cleansed her hands, arms and face, Jacinta's mother gave her a pair of pants and shirt that probably belonged to one of the village boys. She checked on Jacinta and the baby once more before going into the other bedroom to change into the clean clothes.

Lucero showed them to Honoria's home, then bid them good-night. Two kerosene lamps illuminated the tiny shack, casting a warm, golden glow over the interior. The house consisted of one sparsely decorated room. Victoria noticed an old stove, two straight-back chairs and a table with the paint peeling. A cupboard hugged one corner and an iron bedstead graced the other.

Quinn closed the door behind them, then surveyed the room. "Looks like someone fixed us supper." He nodded his head, indicating the two plates on the table.

"I'm not really hungry," she told him. "I think I'll save mine for breakfast. All I want to do is lie down and rest."

He saw her look longingly at the bed. "You take the bed. I'll make a pallet on the floor later."

"You're the one who should take the bed," she told him. "After all, I slept some last night and I'll bet you haven't slept in two nights."

"I catnapped. Besides, there's no way I'm going to take the bed and have you sleep on the floor."

Victoria walked to the bed, leaned over and then ran her hand across the cool, threadbare cotton sheets. With her back to Quinn, she said, "There's room enough for both of us. We could share the bed."

Six

Quinn's stomach tightened. "I don't think our sharing a bed is such a good idea."

"Don't you trust me?" she asked, her lips twitching with the prelude to a smile. She sat on the edge of the bed and removed her boots and socks.

"I don't trust myself," he mumbled, his voice barely audible.

"I'm tired and sleepy, and so are you. We're two adults. We should be able to share a bed without feeling awkward about it. After all, it's not as if I'm inviting you to have sex with me." Victoria turned down the top sheet, then glanced over her shoulder and bestowed a full-blown smile on Quinn. "I'm just suggesting we sleep in the same bed. Sleep and nothing more."

After stretching out on the bed, she studied Quinn, who remained by the door. He seemed to be considering her offer. Curling her index finger, she wriggled it at him in a come-here gesture.

He shook his head. "Go to sleep, princess. I'll join you later."

What was wrong with her big, macho mercenary? she wondered. Had she actually unnerved him by suggesting they share the same bed? The thought of someone as inexperienced as she being able to shake a guy such as Quinn intrigued her. Did she really tempt him? "Promise me you won't sleep on that hard floor." She yawned. Her eyelids fluttered.

"Don't worry about me. I'll be fine." He crossed the room, laid their rifles on the table and then sat. He lifted a banana from the table, peeled it and ate it slowly.

"Promise you'll sleep with me," she said again, her voice weak and groggy.

Her eyelids opened briefly. She glanced his way, then closed her eyes and flipped over onto her side. A soft, settling-in moan escaped her lips. He forced himself to stop staring at her. There was nothing he'd like better than to sleep with her, to hold her in his arms all night and take her again and again.

"Promise," she repeated, the word mixed with another yawn.

"I promise," he said reluctantly.

He was so damned tired and sleepy that it wouldn't take much for him to topple over. He couldn't help glancing back at Victoria one more time, as she lay there in the bed, her eyes closed, her breathing deep and regular. She'd fallen asleep a few minutes after her head hit the pillow.

Just how innocent was Victoria Fortune? he wondered. Did she really think that because they were two adults, they could sleep in the same bed without becoming aroused? If she truly believed that, then she didn't know much about men. Certainly nothing about him.

What he needed, before even attempting to fall asleep at her side, was a long walk. Maybe a stroll around La Luz would clear his head and give him time to rationalize why he shouldn't seduce Victoria. There had to be half a dozen good reasons, if only he could think of them.

Deliberately trying to avoid more thoughts of Victoria, Quinn mulled over their situation and wondered if the villagers had thought of posting some kind of sentry to watch for rebel soldiers. He doubted Esteban's men would attack a village so high in the mountains, but after what had happened at Luquillo, he couldn't rule out the possibility. Since Lucero seemed to be the head man around here, Quinn supposed he should speak to him.

Just as Quinn stepped outside, Alonzo met him. "How is the *señorita?*"

"She's asleep."

"You, too, should be resting, *señor.*"

"I will, but I wanted to check with Lucero about posting a guard tonight. Just in case—"

"It has been done already, *señor.* Two men. One at the east entrance to the village and one at the west," Alonzo explained. "Please know that we are grateful to you and your woman for all your help, but especially for saving Jacinta's life and giving my great-granddaughter a chance to survive. She is all that we have left of Fidel."

Tears on the old man's cheeks glistened in the

moonlight. Quinn had no idea what to say. He didn't know the right words to comfort him.

"If rebel troops do come here, they will learn nothing about you from us," Alonzo said. "We protect our friends."

Quinn shook the old man's hand, then walked with him for a while, until he noticed that Alonzo grew weary. After they parted company, Quinn continued his stroll through the village. Not until complete exhaustion claimed him, did he return to the midwife's house.

Sleeping soundly, Victoria still rested on her side. Why couldn't she be some willing native girl or someone he'd picked up at a local cantina? Quinn thought. Why did she have to be a client?

The bed looked inviting. He was dead on his feet. And she *had* invited him to share the bed, hadn't she? So, why the hell not? After all, he had promised her he wouldn't sleep on the floor. Besides, he was too damn tired to do anything other than sleep.

He removed his boots and socks, then took off his shirt and hung it across a chair. After extinguishing both lights, he crossed the room in his bare feet. He turned down the top sheet and crawled in beside Victoria. Once lying alongside her, he realized the bed was a lot smaller than it looked. He was going to have a damn hard time keeping their bodies from touching during the night. Instantly his sex hardened. He'd never slept with a woman without making love to her.

I'm not inviting you to have sex with me. He heard her words echoing in his mind.

Maybe she didn't think by offering to share the bed with him that she'd issued him an invitation for something more. But he couldn't help wondering what she'd do if he pulled her into his arms and kissed her. Somehow he didn't think she would turn him away.

Get your mind off sex, McCoy, that inner voice warned him. *And go to sleep! Once you've returned her safely to her daddy, you can find yourself a woman. Hell, with half a million dollars, you can buy yourself a harem!*

But the woman he wanted right now was a piece of forbidden fruit. A juicy little red plum just ripe for the picking.

Despite his restlessness, Quinn tried not to move, tried to lie as still as he possibly could. If he touched her, he probably wouldn't be able to stop until he had explored every inch of her sleek body. And once he took her completely, once their relationship changed from client and rescuer to lovers, he would have broken his cardinal rule about not getting sexually involved with a client. Once saving her life became a personal matter, he would lose his impersonal edge in dealing with emergencies. He might be able to claim some other woman without becoming possessive, but not Victoria. He hadn't done more than kiss her and already he had to fight the sense of ownership he felt.

Closing his eyes, Quinn longed for sleep. He

would need all the rest he could get tonight because he'd have to settle for light napping during the upcoming nights. Until they were safely off Santo Bonisto, he would have to remain on guard twenty-four hours a day. Not only did his life depend upon it, but so did Victoria's.

Waking with a start, Victoria shot straight up in bed. A large form lay next to her, its big, hairy arm draped across her belly. Quinn! His deep, loud breathing expressed the depth of his exhaustion.

Moonlight filtered through the thin curtains hanging from the two windows, one on each side of the house. Shadows danced on the dark wooden floor and along the plank walls.

She glanced down at Quinn's arm where it rested across her body. A muscular arm, dusted with brown hair. Her gaze traveled up his arm, noting the pale blue tattoo of an eagle that spread across his bicep. His broad shoulders easily spanned half the width of the bed.

Victoria's fingers itched to touch his chest, to caress his nipples, to curl her fingers in the thatch of hair that rested in the center and dissected his body in two in a line down his belly and inside his unsnapped pants.

Don't even think about it! her mind shouted. *Quinn isn't the kind of man with whom you can play games. If you touch him, you'll wake him. Do you really want to rouse the sleeping beast? Are you prepared to appease his hunger?* No, of course not!

She eased herself from under the weight of his big arm, careful not to disturb him. There was no way she could lie there, so close to him, and not touch his magnificent body. She was, after all, only human. And even if she didn't have a string of ex-lovers, she knew what lust was. Lust was what she felt for Quinn McCoy.

Praying the floor wouldn't squeak as she swung her legs off the bed, she glanced over her shoulder to make sure Quinn was still sleeping. He was. She stood, then walked across the room to look out the window facing east. East to Gurabo. East to safety. Lifting the curtain to the side, she gazed up at the bright, creamy moon that emitted a pale, yellow-white shower of light over the mountain village. Peaceful. Serene. Untouched by war.

Why had she been so stubbornly foolish when her father had first called and begged her to come home? Why hadn't she listened to him? Why had she so arrogantly believed that she could remain in Palmira without becoming a victim of the Santo Bonisto civil war?

Had anyone in Palmira suffered because of her? Had Captain Esteban tortured Dolores or Ernesto as he had Julio Vargas, trying to discover her where-abouts? The very thought that her actions might have caused harm to others bothered her greatly. If she had gone home to Texas weeks ago, would Fidel still be alive? Had her desperation to stay where she believed she was needed caused more harm than good?

"What's wrong?" Quinn asked. "Can't you sleep?"

She jumped and gasped at the sound of his voice, then swerved around to face him. He sat upright in bed, the covers thrown back, his arms braced behind his head. She swallowed hard. Moonlight washed over his lean, muscular body, tinting his tanned flesh with a coppery glow.

"Do you have any idea what time it is?" she asked, willing her rioting senses to calm.

Why couldn't Quinn be less attractive? Why did he have to be so big and macho, so rugged and powerfully built? And why did he, just by looking at her, make her feel so much like a woman, when all the men she'd known before had made her feel like one of the boys?

He pushed a button on his wristwatch and checked the lighted dial. "Nearly one o'clock. We've got a few more hours before we head out. Come back to bed." He patted the mattress.

"I'm not sure I can sleep."

"Did you have a nightmare?" he asked.

She started to say no, but suddenly realized that she had, indeed, had a nightmare. A frightening dream that had wakened her. Only fragments of the dream remained clear in her mind. Quinn surrounded by a horde of rebel troops. Guns firing. Blood spreading out on the ground. Quinn's blood!

Shuddering, she hunched over and covered her face with her hand. Tears lodged in her throat as a surreal foreboding encompassed her. Had the dream been a premonition? Was Quinn fated to die by trying to save her? She gasped loudly, unable to bear the thought of anything happening to him.

The thud of his feet hitting the wooden floor gained her immediate attention. She lifted her head and stared directly at him. Overwhelmingly manly in nothing but his rumpled khaki pants, he stood beside the bed and watched her.

"Want to tell me about it?" he asked. "It might make you feel better."

"I'm not sure anything can make me feel better," she admitted. "If I could undo what happened to Fidel and Julio and God knows how many other people, then I might feel better."

"So that's it." He walked toward her, halting when only a couple of feet separated them. "Stop beating yourself up over what happened to Julio and Fidel. It wasn't your fault. This country is at war and they were casualties of the war."

"If Captain Esteban hadn't been searching for me—"

Lighting-fast, Quinn reached out and grabbed her. His action startled her, but she made no protest when he wrapped his arms around her and pressed her head down on his chest. She hadn't realized until the very moment it happened, how much she longed to be in his arms. His big, strong, comforting arms.

"Don't play the 'if' game, honey. You can never win." While he caressed her back with one hand, he lifted the other and massaged her neck. "You aren't responsible for the world's ills any more than you can cure all of them. You're just one little ole gal from Texas, who happens to have a big heart and an overpowering desire to help people.''

"Oh, Quinn, you're giving me more credit than I deserve.'' She closed her eyes, savoring the warmth of his body, the heady musky scent of his skin and the cocoon of safety in which he encompassed her.

"I don't think so,'' he said. "You genuinely care about people. You seem to be able to relate to everyone on a personal level, as if you understand how they feel. It seems to be your nature to want to help everybody.''

"I should have listened to my father weeks ago when he tried to persuade me to come home. My stubbornness could cost you your life.''

His stroking fingers crept up into her hair. She sighed. He cupped the back of her head.

"Is that what the dream was about? Did you dream I got killed?''

She eased her arms around his waist and clung to him. "I don't want you to die. I don't want—''

Putting pressure on her neck, he forced her head up to lift her mouth to his. Her lips parted on an expectant sigh. He swooped down, taking her mouth in a breath-robbing kiss. Without hesitation, she responded. She wanted this, needed this, as she had never before wanted or needed anything.

For the life of her, she couldn't figure out any rational explanation for the way she felt about Quinn. Lust, definitely. Something more, certainly. But what that something more was, she didn't know.

While his mouth ravaged hers, his big hand held her head in place, a captive of his strength. He caressed her buttocks through the cotton material of her pants, his hand insistent and demanding.

Her nipples tightened. Her breasts swelled. Her femininity clenched and unclenched, shooting tingles of anticipation through her body.

Entangled together, their bodies straining for closer contact, Quinn and Victoria explored each other with lips and fingertips. She loved the feel of his naked chest and back. She found power and strength in his hard, disciplined body. Her lips planted a row of kisses across his chest. He licked a trail down her neck. When he unbuttoned her shirt, she held her breath. His heated gaze fondled her with urgent hunger. Then he cupped one breast, allowing his thumb to lightly rub across her erect nipple. Reveling in his touch, she tossed back her head and sighed.

When his mouth sought her breast, she cupped his head, holding him against her body, encouraging him. As he laved her breast, he slid his hand inside the loose waistband of her borrowed slacks.

She shuddered as sensations unlike anything she'd ever known vibrated inside her.

Quinn massaged her naked buttocks, his big, open palm caressing. He knew she was unraveling under his passionate attention. But this little taste of her wasn't enough. He wanted more. He wanted it all.

Not thinking about the consequences, urged on by his desire, he swept her up into his arms and carried her to the bed. When he came down over her, she looked up at him and he saw the same passion that rode him so hard reflected in her eyes. She was as aroused and needy as he.

Quinn hovered over her, his eyes feasting on her exposed breasts. She reached for him, her fingers hesitant.

"I don't know what I'm doing," she told him.

He stilled, his rapid breath warm on her naked flesh. "Are you having second thoughts about our making love?"

"No, no second thoughts," she said. "It's just that I'm unsure about my ability to please you. I'm not experienced at this."

"Just looking at you pleases me." He kissed her belly. Her breath caught in her throat. "Just touching you pleases me." He lifted his head and smiled at her. "Actually I'm glad you've had only two or three lovers instead of two or three dozen."

She quivered under his touch. To halt his further exploration, she clasped his hand. "You don't understand, Quinn." She had to tell him, didn't she? He had a right to know just how inexperienced she was. "I haven't had two or three lovers." She hesitated when she noted the surprised look on his face. "To be honest, I haven't had even one."

She felt his withdrawal before he actually shoved himself up and off the bed. He glowered down at her where she lay, vulnerable and trembling. Suddenly she realized that she shouldn't have told him.

She should have let him discover the fact for himself. Apparently he had no desire to initiate a virgin.

Victoria pulled her shirt together, then buttoned it. After easing to the side of the bed, she stood. Quinn watched her as she walked toward him. The closer she came the more tense his muscles grew, until he felt as if he were made of stone. His body ached with need. He wanted this woman and he wanted her now. His mind raged against him for letting things go so far. Why hadn't he listened to his common sense and kept his relationship with her strictly business? But somewhere deep inside him, in an unknown place, he experienced a purely male exhilaration at the thought Victoria was a virgin and she wanted him to be her first lover.

"Does my being a virgin change things between us?" she asked.

He held up both hands in a gesture for her to stop, to not come any closer. "It's my fault things went as far as they did," he told her. "I knew better than to... I don't have sex with my clients. Getting involved with a woman tends to muddle a man's brain and affects his actions when there's danger. When a guy lets his body do his thinking then he's in trouble."

"You don't want me?" She gazed pleadingly at him, needing his reassurance. "If I weren't a virgin and I weren't your client, then would you make love to me?"

He balled his hands into fists to keep himself from reaching for her. Didn't she have any idea just how much he wanted her? God, she was completely in-experienced if she didn't realize that he'd walk over hot coals for the right to take her. He couldn't re-member the last time he'd wanted a woman so much. Maybe never.

"I want you," he admitted. "But you and me—" he flipped his index finger toward her and then back at himself "—are an event that isn't going to hap-pen. I'm a real bad boy. My type makes a lousy first lover for a girl like you. If you've saved yourself all these years, then you're obviously waiting for prince charming. Believe me, I'm no prince."

"Then I didn't make a fool of myself? You don't think I threw myself at you?"

Despite the way Quinn's body still ached with desire, he managed a weak smile. "I'm the one who made a fool of himself, not realizing that you're a virgin princess and I'm just a horny toad who can't be changed into a prince with a magic kiss."

"I'm embarrassed," she told him. "I don't know what it is about you that attracts me so, but every time I look at you, I get weak in the knees. And the crazy thing is that, until today, I didn't even like you."

Quinn chuckled. "Yeah, I know. To be totally honest, I didn't like you all that much, either, so there's no need to be embarrassed. Let's just chalk up what happened to unwanted sexual attraction and the dangerous situation we're in."

Victoria hugged herself as she rocked back and

forth on her bare heels. "I suppose we should try to get a little more sleep tonight."

"Yeah." Quinn glanced across the room. "You take the bed. I'll toss a pillow and blanket on the floor."

"You should take the—"

"Don't argue with me. Go to bed."

She nodded. "Just to set the record straight—you may not be prince charming, but you're not a toad, either."

He waited until she crawled into bed before he removed one of the pillows and one of the blankets. After taking the items to the far side of the room, he prepared himself a makeshift pallet and then settled in for what was left of the night. Restless and still partially aroused, he tossed back and forth on the hard floor.

He had to get her off this damn island and back to her father in Texas as soon as possible. If the rebel soldiers didn't wind up killing him, then there was a good chance his desire for Victoria Fortune would.

Victoria left La Luz reluctantly, despite the fact that she knew she couldn't do any more for little Bella than the women of the village. Without the equipment in a prenatal unit, only God could keep the tiny infant alive. So the most Victoria could do, under the circumstances, was pray.

From now until she returned home, her top priority was doing whatever was necessary to keep

Quinn and her alive. That meant a trek down the mountain and through the treacherous jungle. The roads, even the minor dirt trails, would be more likely pathways for the rebel soldiers. Another part of surviving meant obeying Quinn's orders, no matter what. She had promised herself that she wouldn't argue with his authority, ever again. Nothing and no one was going to interfere with their reaching Gurabo as soon as possible.

Their journey down the eastern slope of Mt. Simona began smoothly. And despite the clouds to the north, the day was sunny. Quinn found a descending spiral trial and followed it for several miles, then the path led to an open road, which he wanted to avoid. So he chose to hack a new path through the jungle. Having to clear a walkway as they traveled slowed them down considerably.

The monkeys and birds, common to the jungle, eluded Victoria's gaze while she concentrated on keeping pace with Quinn as they became immersed in the mountainside forest. Occasionally a small lizard darted across their path or large morpho butterflies fluttered by, their iridescent blue wings like glass in the sunlight.

They took frequent breaks, for which she was grateful, and knew those rest stops were for her sake and not Quinn's. He seemed to possess superhuman strength and an inexhaustible supply of energy. She supposed both were a result of years of experience and routine training to keep in top physical shape.

With the sun's position in the sky announcing

high noon even before Quinn checked his watch, Victoria began searching for a place where they could stop. As if she had conjured up the spot, a clearing appeared in front of them. Upon closer inspection they found the ruins of an old building. Numerous stones lay in haphazard disarray around the few feet of the structure that remained intact. Grass, heavy vines and small shrubs appeared to be doing their best to reclaim the crumbling mass.

She waited patiently while Quinn checked the area for unwelcome snakes. One wall, now only a couple of feet high, seemed fairly sturdy when Quinn tested it, so they removed their backpacks, propped their rifles against the wall and sat on the uneven ledge. They drank from their canteens, but since neither of them were hungry, they decided to wait until later to eat.

Victoria excused herself and went several feet into the thicket. She glanced around hurriedly, then went about her business. Just as she pulled up her pants, she heard a noise.

"Quinn?" she whispered.

No response. But there was the noise again, as if someone or something was scampering over the underbrush. Oh, God, what if it was a rebel soldier? She had to get back to Quinn as fast as possible.

"Quinn!" This time she screamed his name.

When she whirled around, intending to return to the clearing, the sound grew louder. Whatever it was, it was coming right at her. Where was Quinn? Why hadn't he seen the intruder?

Her heart fluttered uncontrollably as thoughts of Quinn lying dead on the ground flashed through her mind. Had a rebel soldier or perhaps more than one sneaked up on Quinn and knocked him over the head? No, that wasn't possible. Quinn would never have been taken unawares.

Suddenly the thing—the large, hairy creature— broke through the thicket and came directly at her. She screamed, the sound echoing. She started to run, but realized the beast was too close, she'd never outrun it. Dammit, why had she left her rifle back at the ruins? Her gaze darted in every direction, seeking a means of escape. Without giving her actions a second thought, she rushed to a nearby tree and began an awkward climb. As a kid, she had scaled trees with her brothers and generally run amuck on the ranch, every bit as much of a little hellion as her brothers had been. But it had been years since she'd climbed a tree.

Her foot slipped. She slid down, down, down. When her butt forcefully hit the ground, she cried out in pain. Her eyes widened in horror as all two hundred pounds of raging boar zeroed in on her.

"Quinn!"

The gun blast obliterated her last cry for help. The one shot hit its mark. The animal dropped dead only inches from her feet. She released the breath she'd been holding.

Quinn inspected the huge hog, then bent and offered Victoria a hand. She accepted his offer, allowing him to help her to her feet. He draped the M-16 over his shoulder, then pulled her to his side.

She clung to him, knowing she would always find a safe haven in his arms. Her heartbeat still raced at breakneck speed. Perspiration dampened her face. "That thing could have killed me. Look at those tusks!" Tears of relief misted her eyes. She lifted her trembling fingers and grabbed his shirtfront.

He glanced over at the dead animal. "Wild hogs can be dangerous." He kissed her lightly on the temple. "But you don't have anything to worry about now." Quinn soothed her, running his hand up and down her back as he made comforting sounds deep in his throat. "Shhh, hush. It's all over. You're safe."

"Where were you when I cried out? I was afraid something had happened to you."

He encompassed her within his embrace, hoping she would feel secure. As he stroked her tenderly, the tremors in her body began to subside and she curled herself around him like a tabby cat around its master's leg.

"I'd gone off to do the same thing you were doing," he explained. "When I heard you scream, I came as quickly as I could." He glanced meaningfully at his unzipped pants.

Oddly enough Victoria found the sight of his open fly hilarious. She chuckled softly several times, then burst out laughing. "Oh, Quinn. You were just off watering the grass and I was afraid rebel soldiers had slit your throat.'' Her laughter escalated until it became an almost hysterical cry.

Quinn realized that she couldn't stop laughing, that she was experiencing the aftereffects of panic. If he didn't end her uncontrolled outburst, she'd soon start hyperventilating.

He could slap her, he could shake her, or he could do the unexpected and take her by surprise. He preferred the latter. He couldn't imagine any circumstances that would cause him to lay a hurtful hand on her.

Pulling her intimately against him, he ravaged her mouth, silencing the laughter. He deepened the kiss, thrusting his tongue, exploring the welcome warmth inside. She moaned. The last remnants of fear and panic drained from her body and mind. He felt the release as surely as if he were a part of her.

He ended the kiss. She gazed soberly up into his concerned eyes. Lifting her hand to his face, she caressed his beard-stubbled cheek. ''My hero.''

''Don't go from hysterical to silly.'' He shoved her gently out of his arms. ''Come on. Let's get moving. We can still cover quite a few miles before nightfall.''

She grabbed his arm. ''Are you going to leave that thing there?'' She glanced at the feral hog. ''I mean, can't we use it for food?''

''We can, if you want to eat it raw.''

''Oh. I'd forgotten. No fires. Smoke can be seen for miles.''

''Yeah, and gunshots can be heard for miles.''

"Damn! Do you suppose—"

"It couldn't be helped." He pulled free of her hold. "Let's make tracks, honey."

Without another word, she followed him into the clearing. They put on their backpacks, replenished with food and water in La luz, then she lifted her rifle from where it rested against the wall. Quinn led the way, slicing a path through the jungle, heading down the mountain toward Gurabo.

Had someone heard the rifle shot when Quinn had killed the boar? she wondered. Would they encounter trouble before they camped for the night? Or would trouble wait for tomorrow?

Seven

How could it be morning? Victoria wondered. It was still dark, wasn't it? She could use another two or three hours of sleep. But Quinn hurried her, pointing out the ominous gray clouds overhead when he told her it was six-thirty. He explained that if they hurried, they might outrun the rain that was heading this way.

"The rain's coming in from the north and should get here any time now. Since we're going east, we should see sunshine most of the day."

Grumbling to herself, she roused quickly and jumped to her feet. Considering the situation—spending the night in the jungle and not knowing if another band of rebels would appear out of no-where—they had both slept fully clothed and with their boots on.

"We should make the Rio Gurabo by early afternoon and hopefully be able to beg, borrow or steal a boat of some sort," he said.

"If?" She'd definitely heard an implied "if" at the end of his sentence.

"*If* our luck holds out and we don't have any problems today."

"I assume there's a village near the Rio Gurabo since you intend to *borrow* a boat to go downriver."

"Actually there are several villages along the Rio Gurabo, so if we don't find a boat at one place, we can make our way to the second and even the third village, if necessary. And if we confiscate a boat, we could be in Gurabo by tonight and off this damn island by morning."

"Sounds too easy, doesn't it?"

"Shut your mouth, woman!" Quinn teased. "No negative thoughts."

"We will make it to Gurabo tonight. We will make it to Gurabo tonight." Victoria transformed the sentence into a chant.

"Hungry?" he asked.

"Ravenous," she replied. "But I'd skip food for the rest of the day if I could only have a bath."

"Yeah, I know what you mean." He surveyed her rumpled clothes, stained with perspiration and dirt, then glanced down at his own disheveled state. He rubbed his open palm over the three days' growth of beard darkening his face. "We're both pretty scruffy, aren't we?"

She ran her tongue across her teeth, then made a disgusted face. "My teeth feel like they've got mold growing on them." Spearing her fingers through her short hair, she groaned.

"Eat some fruit and rinse your mouth with water," he suggested. "That'll help some. Once we get to Gurabo, you can soak in a tub of hot water for as long as you'd like."

"Ah, that sounds like heaven."

Quinn opened his backpack, removed a couple of apples, then tossed one to her. "I've been saving these. You've been such a good girl, I think you need a treat this morning."

After catching the apple, she brought it immediately to her mouth and took a huge bite.

Quinn ate hurriedly, then tossed the apple core into the brush and wiped his hands on his pants. After opening his canteen, he downed a swig of water. While he waited for Victoria to finish her breakfast, he withdrew the compass from his pocket and checked directions. He had a sixth sense when it came to directions and had never gotten lost—not ever. But he always backed up his instincts by regularly checking his compass and studying a map of the area.

"I'm ready." Victoria put on her backpack, picked up the M-1 and marched over to Quinn. "Let's move out."

"Who's giving the orders here, Ms. Fortune?" He grinned at her. With her face totally void of makeup, her hair stringy and her baggy, borrowed clothes soiled, Victoria looked like a grungy little girl who'd been outside playing all day and was ready for an evening bath. But beneath those loose pants and shirt he knew was the body of a woman— a woman he wanted. "Stay close and be ready to jump if I give the order."

"Yes, sir!"

Victoria fell into step behind him, all the while

enjoying the view of his big body as he stalked through the jungle, clearing a path for her. Soon blue skies spread out overhead, with only an errant white cloud here and there. As Quinn had predicted, they'd left the dark clouds and rain showers higher up in the mountains.

As they progressed steadily down the side of the mountain, the slopes became steep and the path narrowed. On her left side, she could reach out and touch the mountainside and if she made one false move to the right, she could fall over the edge to her death.

"Be very careful along here," Quinn said. "There's a hundred-foot drop to your right." He grabbed hold of a tree root protruding from the mountainside. "Use the trees and the roots to help balance yourself."

Victoria held her breath, then followed Quinn, obeying his instructions as they maneuvered the deadly incline. With each passing day, each passing hour, each passing moment, she admired Quinn more and more. His expertise had gotten her this far and she didn't doubt that it would get her all the way to Gurabo and then safely home to Texas.

She could hardly wait to see her father. To thank him. And to thank Sam Waterman, too, for recommending Quinn to her father. She'd have to tell her father that he had more than gotten his money's worth from the mercenary he'd hired to rescue her.

The farther they descended Mt. Simona, the more the angle of the slopes leveled out. The forest floor cleared somewhat and tall trees, including several blue mahoe, towered above them.

She breathed a sigh of relief to finally be able to walk without clutching to tree roots while praying not to lose her footing. Quinn stopped abruptly, prompting her to halt. Were they going to take a break? she hoped. The hazardous climb along the mountain ridge had taken a lot out of her. She could use a few minutes of down time before they trudged on toward the river.

Suddenly, Quinn grabbed her, and shoved her to the ground as he dropped down on his belly. A sniper shot quickly ended her brief moment of relaxation.

Where were the shots coming from and who was firing on them? she wondered. Rebel troops? Or possibly Nationalist soldiers?

"Follow me," Quinn ordered. "And keep your head down."

They crawled, then rolled, trampling the underbrush and smashing through a thicket. Bullets sailed over their heads and zipped alongside their bodies.

"Over there." Quinn nodded to the grove of mountain guava trees. "My guess is there's at least four of them. Maybe five."

"Five!" she cried out softly.

"You're going to have to keep them occupied, while I go around behind them," he said. "Do you think you can do that?"

"I don't know…I—I… Yes, I can do it." Victoria swallowed her fear. "I have to, don't I?"

He nodded, then leaned over and kissed her on the head. "Start returning their fire the minute I leave. Hopefully, they didn't notice we both had weapons and they'll think only one of us has a rifle."

On her belly in the grass, the butt of the M-1 resting on her shoulder, Victoria took aim and began firing into the grove of guava trees. A loud yelp and then a crash told her that she'd hit someone. Her heart stopped beating for a split second at the thought that she, a nurse trained to save lives, might have just ended one.

But this wasn't a hospital or a clinic. This was the jungle. Those men firing at her had no qualms about killing her. And if she didn't keep a steady stream of bullets heading toward the enemy, it would lessen Quinn's chances of sneaking up on them from behind.

She tried not to think about Quinn either killing or being killed. The thought of losing Quinn was unbearable.

Creeping through the forest, Quinn circled around to the back of the five men he could now make out plainly through the high grass and dense brush. One man lay on the ground bleeding. Victoria's gunfire must have hit him. She was probably over there feeling all kinds of guilt for having taken another human being's life. That was the kind of person she was.

He was sure, if she had anything to say about the situation, she would prefer for him to take these men hostage. But that wasn't an option. Four men to guard on their journey to Gurabo would be suicide. And if he tied them up—if he could find enough rope—and left them here, another ragtag group of roaming soldiers might stumble across them and free them. Then Esteban and Xavier would have a damn good idea where he and Victoria were and they'd be sure to send out troops to follow their path. No, this was definitely a "kill or be killed" scenario.

Putting aside the mental debate, Quinn removed the scope from his backpack, attached it to his rifle and then used the backpack as support for the M-16. With deadly precision and experience, he aimed his weapon. Unaware of the danger behind them, the soldiers continued firing at Victoria. Quinn took the rebels by surprise. Methodically, in rapid-fire motion, he mowed them down, while only the last two were able to return fire. Within minutes the battle was over, Quinn the easy victor.

Nausea rose in his stomach. Bile burned a trail up his esophagus and into his throat. He was a trained professional who'd never enjoyed killing, but he always did what had to be done. It had been years since he'd gone into combat and killed, years that had chiseled away at his ability to kill without regret.

After wiping his mouth with the back of his hand, he grabbed his rifle, draped it over his right shoulder and picked up his backpack. Across the clearing, still hidden in the thicket, Victoria continued firing. He crept through the forest, retracing his steps. Slinging the backpack over his left shoulder, he listened to the echoes of Victoria's last shots. Apparently she realized that the rebel troops were no longer attacking.

Quinn dreaded seeing the look in her eyes when she realized that he'd killed the other four men. He didn't want her to see him as a ruthless killer, but could someone like Victoria—a healer—understand his reasons for wiping out the ragtag group of soldiers? For the life of him, he couldn't figure out why he cared what she thought of him. Never before had a woman's opinion of him mattered one way or the other.

Pausing when he saw her lying on the ground, still on her belly, her hands glued to the M-1, he realized she was too scared to move.

"Victoria?"

She wheeled around and aimed the rifle directly at him. "Quinn?" Her gaze traveled the length of his body, from head to toe, then she studied the expression on his face. "You're all right." She lowered her rifle.

"Yeah, honey, I'm okay. How about you?"

She looked as scared as a green recruit during his first battle. But as the trouper he knew her to be, she'd done what he'd asked of her and kept the rebel soldiers occupied while he'd positioned himself for the attack.

"The soldiers?" she asked.

"They're all dead."

"All of them?"

"There were five."

"I—I killed one of them, didn't I?" She struggled to her feet, then dropped the M-1 to the ground. "I've never killed anyone before."

"Remember, this is war and in war it's either kill or be killed," Quinn reminded her. "What you did and what I did, saved our lives."

"I understand." With her shoulders slumped and her head bowed, she dropped to her knees. She gasped in large gulps of air, then let out a loud, mournful cry.

Quinn couldn't get to her fast enough. He'd known the aftermath was going to be rough on her, had known she'd be consumed with guilt and sorrow. When he took her in his arms, she clung to him and sobbed uncontrollably against his chest. He allowed her a few minutes to release the tension, then he grabbed her by the shoulders and forced her to face him.

"We can't hang around here…in case there are any more soldiers nearby." When she only stared at him with glazed eyes, he shook her gently. "The exchange of gunfire would have alerted anyone in the area. We should get going. Now."

"But what about those men? Aren't we going to bury them?" Her misty green eyes pleaded.

Squeezing her shoulders, he shook his head. "We can't take the time. We need to keep moving."

"Yes, of course, you're right."

He picked up the M-1, handed it to her and then cupped her chin with his hand. "You'll be okay, won't you?"

She nodded. "I'm glad I didn't see them—the soldiers we killed."

"Don't think about them. Concentrate on something else," he told her. "Think about being home with your family. Keep your mind focused on returning to the Double Crown Ranch and how good it'll be to see your father again."

Taking her hand, Quinn guided her for several yards, back onto the downward trail. When he released her hand, she fell into step behind him. They continued descending the eastern ridge of Mt. Simona at an accelerated pace, Victoria forcing herself to keep up with Quinn. She knew why he forged ahead in such a frenzy. They had to stay one step ahead of any rebels who might have heard the gunplay and could at this very moment be tracking them.

A good two hours later Quinn slowed his pace, then halted briefly and glanced back at her. "How are you holding up? Do you think you can make it a few more miles before resting?"

With her lungs aching, her feet sore and her legs crying out for rest, she forced a smile, nodded and said, "A few more miles."

He took in her brightly flushed cheeks, her heaving chest and heard the breathlessness in her voice. Victoria couldn't go another yard, let alone a few more miles. Despite being in good condition, better than most women under similar circumstances, she didn't have the stamina to keep up with him.

"I'm thirsty," he said as he walked toward her.

Before he reached her, he took off his backpack and removed his canteen. "We'll take our break now."

"No, please, Quinn, don't stop because of me. I told you that I can make it a few more miles."

He held the canteen up to her lips. "Shut up and drink."

She guzzled down the tepid water. When she finished, Quinn poured a handful into his palm, then splashed it on her face. With the tips of his fingers, he wiped off the excess. He removed her knapsack and dropped it beside his on the ground.

"Five minutes and then we head out again," he told her as he sat and crossed one leg under the other. "Come on down." He grasped her wrist and tugged her onto his lap.

When she fell into the cradle of his legs, she grabbed at thin air, then circled his neck with her arms and stared wide-eyed into his smiling face. "I'm sorry that I'm slowing us down. I'm doing the best I can, but—"

He placed his index finger across her lips. "You're doing great, princess. I know you're giving it everything you've got. Nobody could ask for a better partner under these circumstances."

"You really mean that, don't you?" Sighing, she leaned her head on his shoulder and closed her eyes. "I need to rest for just a minute." Quinn was so good to her, she thought. He was taking care of her when she couldn't take care of herself. She loved the feeling of protection she found in his arms.

Sitting there on the damp earth, a South American

forest and a full-blown civil war surrounding them, Quinn held Victoria. Moments ticked by in complete silence, only the distinct, muted sounds of the jungle permeating the air. Ten minutes passed without either of them saying a word. Quinn wondered if she had fallen asleep. But when he shifted his legs, she stirred to life and lifted her head to look at him.

"We've been here too long, haven't we?" she asked.

He checked his watch. "Less than fifteen minutes."

Leaving the nest of his embrace was one of the most difficult things she'd ever done, but she had no choice. Quinn had indulged her weakness long enough. She forced herself to stand.

"I'll be all right now."

"You're sure?"

Within minutes they resumed their positions and continued on toward the Rio Gurabo. The sun beamed bright and hot, its rays filtering through the gradually thinning canopy of tree branches as the terrain leveled off even more.

Quinn heard water flowing, and when he turned to tell Victoria that a stream was close by, she smiled at him.

"I hear it, too," she said. "I don't suppose we can stop for a bath?"

"We can stop only long enough to eat a bite and wash off," he told her. "Once we reach the Rio Gurabo, you can dive in and take a bath."

"Fair enough. I suppose I can wait a few more hours."

"Maybe less," he said. "If my estimations are correct, we're only about an hour from the river."

"Hooray and hallelujah."

With perspiration dampening their skin and exhaustion playing havoc with every muscle in their bodies, they accelerated their pace, heading toward the sound of the water.

Knowing how she longed to wash off, even if just her face and hands, Quinn moved aside to allow Victoria to reach the shallow, almost dry stream first. No doubt the source of this small stream was some underground spring, he thought, as was the source of most streams on Santo Bonisto. He decided that while Victoria enjoyed the cool spring water, he'd rummage in his backpack to see what food supplies they had left and to check the map again.

Victoria couldn't wait to wade in the stream, to bend and fill her hands with water and maybe even douse her head, if she could find a spot that was deep enough. With her thoughts focused on being able to wash away some of the dirt and grime from her body, she didn't pay any attention to the soil that separated the streambed from the bank. Suddenly, without any warning, the ground beneath her feet rippled and shifted.

What the heck was going on?

Within two seconds she sank to her waist in a

liquid quagmire. *Don't panic! Don't panic! Oh, God, help me!*

"Quinn!"

He jerked around at the sound of his name, then seeing what had happened, rushed toward Victoria. "Damn!"

"Do something. Quick. Before I drown in this stuff."

"Try to stay calm," he said. "I'll get you out."

"Hurry."

"Hell! You've got on your backpack and you're wearing boots, so the weight from those are dragging you down," he told her. "Look, honey, do exactly what I tell you to do. Dump your rifle and then see if you can loosen your backpack. You need to get rid of all the extra weight you can."

She eased the rifle from her shoulder, then watched as it disappeared into the quagmire. When she loosened the straps of her backpack, it slid off her back and down into the murky depths.

"Good girl," Quinn called to her. "Now, lie back and distribute your weight evenly over the surface."

"Lie back? Are you kidding?"

"Trust me, Victoria. I know how to deal with quicksand."

Quicksand! She'd been afraid that's what she'd fallen into. And just when she'd thought nothing else could happen, that they might have gotten lucky. "I trust you, Quinn." *I trust you with my life,* she added silently. Immediately she lay back and began floating.

"Whatever you do, don't struggle. Slowly and carefully pull your legs free. Take deep breaths, honey. Filling your lungs with air will make you more buoyant."

She sucked in deep breaths, while Quinn tested the ground at the edge of the streambed. When he figured out where the quicksand began, he braced his feet on solid ground, then employed the "safe" function on his M-16 and held the rifle out to her. "See if you can grab hold."

She reached out, but her fingertips couldn't quite reach the rifle butt. She tried again. Her fingertips brushed the butt, but slid off quickly.

"Try again," he told her.

When she reached out a third time, her nails scraped the end of butt. She clawed into it, but couldn't hold on tightly enough.

"Don't exhaust yourself." He lifted the rifle. "Rest for a couple of seconds before you try again."

"Am I going to drown in this stuff?" She didn't want to die buried in quicksand.

"No, you're not going to drown. It'll just take a while to get you out. Believe me, you'll laugh about this experience later."

"I doubt that!"

"Come on, let's try again." He held out the rifle butt to her.

Her fingers gripped the edge. Holding on with dear life, she dragged herself by slow degrees through the runny quicksand until she was able to grab hold securely.

"I've got it!" she yelled.

"Hang on." Quinn cautiously reeled her in, careful not to lose his footing and fall in himself.

Walking backward as he inched her out of the slush, Quinn grinned. When she stepped onto firm ground, she released the rifle butt and sank to her knees. Quinn chuckled. She jerked her head up and glowered at him.

"What's so damn funny?" she demanded.

"You are, princess. You should see yourself."

With slime dripping off of her from head to toe, she rose from the ground and tramped toward Quinn. He started backing up in an effort to avoid her attack. She hurled herself into him full-force, almost knocking him over, but he grabbed her shoulders and steadied them both. Mud from her clothes stuck to his. Muck clung to her and then to him when she wrapped her arms around his waist.

Looking up at him with devilment in her eyes, she said, "Now you're almost as filthy as I am."

"What we both need is a good bath. And I think I know just the place."

Her eyes widened with hope. "Where?"

"I checked the map while you were falling waist-deep into the bog and I'd say we're less than three miles from the Rio Gurabo."

"Don't kid me. I don't think I could take it."

"I'm not kidding." He shoved her away, then raked the top layer of mud and muck from his clothes.

"What are you waiting for? Lead the way!"

Quinn surveyed her from the top of her grimy hair, down her wet, grubby body to her mud-caked feet. She was a sorry sight, but even this way, he found her immensely appealing. What the hell was wrong with him? How was it possible that regardless of the way she looked, he thought she was the prettiest thing he'd ever seen?

While she waited impatiently, trying to wring some of the muck from her hair and clothes, Quinn gathered up his backpack, strapped it on and slung the M-16 over his shoulder.

"Don't go jumping in as soon as we get there," he said. "Let me check out the area first."

"Don't worry. I've learned my lesson."

Immediately, Victoria fell into step behind him once more, while visions of the Rio Gurabo danced in her head. Three more miles and she could take a bath. Three more miles and they'd be only a few hours from Gurabo. A few hours from the American embassy. A few hours from a plane ride home.

Please, God, don't let anything else go wrong, she prayed.

Eight

Splashing water, gleeful giggles and occasional sighs of delight echoed from the secluded lagoon, a formation from the backwaters of the Rio Gurabo. Quinn had discovered the hidden site while scouting the area when they'd arrived half an hour earlier. The nearest village was a good four miles upstream and from what he could tell no one had been through this particular tract of land recently. The place was as secure as any on Santo Bonisto could be in the midst of war, so he was sure they could wash and rest here in relative safety.

A stand of giant bamboo that canopied a small section of the banks swayed slightly in the humid afternoon breeze. Several orange trees, no doubt planted by farmers in this area years ago, mingled with the shrubs and grass. One lone breadfruit tree towered above the shorter greenery. At least they wouldn't go hungry, Quinn thought.

From his position on a rise above the lagoon, Quinn looked out over the Rio Gurabo, trying his best to keep his mind off the fact that Victoria was cavorting naked only a few yards away. She had asked if it would be safe for her to remove her clothes before diving into the lagoon. When he'd answered in the affirmative, she'd made him promise to keep his back to her while standing guard. For his sake as much as hers, he'd tried to keep that promise. But the desire for one quick glimpse of her shapely, long-legged body grew stronger with each passing moment. Sooner or later, he was going to take a forbidden look and he damn well knew it. The more she splashed and frolicked, the more aroused he became.

He'd be down there with her right now, if she wasn't a client. *Yeah, sure,* chided the voice of reason. Time for total honesty, Quinn conceded. The truth? He wasn't sharing a bath with Victoria because she was a virgin. He was afraid that if he had sex with her, she would think there was more to it. She'd start making plans for the future. A girl who had saved herself for the right man would expect a lot from him—things such as marriage and kids. Apprehension shuttered through Quinn. A sure warning. *Look, but don't touch.*

Telling himself that one quick glance wouldn't hurt either of them, he reversed positions so that he faced the lagoon. His gaze traveled over the surface of the water, slowly but surely seeking and finding the lone occupant. She bounced up and down, her body almost waist-deep, exposing most of her torso to his view. Waterdrops glistened on her face, shoulders and breasts as the sunlight struck them. Quinn breathed deeply as his eyes feasted on her high, firm peaks, their rosy nipples tight and pointed.

When his sex hardened painfully, he cursed himself for a fool. *Stop torturing yourself!* Forcing himself to look away, he stomped down the rise, careful not to glance directly at the lagoon again. She'd been in there long enough, he grumbled to himself. He'd tell her to get out now and let him clean up. They didn't need to waste too much time before heading downstream to the first village. He just hoped they could find an unguarded boat. Without a boat, it would take three times as long to reach Gurabo.

"Hurry up, princess," Quinn called to her. "We can't stay here all day."

"I'll be out in a few minutes," she said. "I never knew how glorious a bath could be."

After retrieving some oranges from the small grove of trees, Quinn stuffed a few into his backpack and laid four on the ground for them to eat while they were here. *Keep busy until she's out of the water and dressed,* instructed the voice. *Think about the trip downriver. Concentrate on the job of getting Victoria back to Texas.*

"It's all yours," she told him.

Quinn snapped around, prepared to tell her it was about time, but one look at her and he couldn't say a word. Apparently she had washed her clothes and put them back on still wet. The thin, cotton pants and shirt she wore, almost transparent in their damp state, clung to her body, accentuating every luscious curve.

"What's wrong?" she asked as she combed her

fingers through her moist hair. "Why are you looking at me like that?"

"Like what?" He could barely get the words past the lump in his throat.

"I don't know, all oddlike, as if I'd sprouted horns or something."

"Nothing like that. I was just thinking how beautiful you are."

"Me?" A blush crept up her neck and covered her face, highlighting her cheeks. Despite the fact she was an identical twin to her beautiful sister Vanessa, Victoria had never considered herself beautiful. Where Vanessa possessed a fragile, china-doll beauty, the same features and traits that belonged to Victoria translated into a fresh, wholesome cuteness.

"Yeah, you," he said.

He tried not to devour her with his gaze, but heaven help him, he couldn't take his eyes off her as she walked toward him. Stronger men than he would be tempted to ravage that deliciously sweet body. As she bent to pick up her boots and damp socks, his heart skipped a beat and his hands itched to reach out and grab her.

When she came up to him, he handed her the M-16. "Your turn to keep watch while I clean up."

She slung the rifle across her shoulder. "You're going to love it."

He began stripping immediately, tossing his shirt on the grassy bank. Victoria averted her gaze just as he reached down to remove his boots. In a couple of minutes, he'd be naked and she didn't think she could look at him without wanting him. And it wasn't that she'd never seen a naked man before—she had. Just not one who looked like Quinn Mc-Coy. And certainly not one she wanted to become her first lover.

Marching away from the sound of water splashing as he entered the lagoon, Victoria tried to guide her thoughts away from how he must look totally naked. *Think about how lucky you are to be alive. Think about how good you feel after your bath. Think about…fantasize about being in Quinn's arms, about lying beneath him and having him enter your body.* The image became so real in her mind that she could almost feel the powerful thrust of his sex as he claimed her.

Victoria stood fifteen feet from the lagoon, her eyes closed, her body quivering. In that one moment out of time, she realized that somewhere along the way, she had fallen in love with her rescuer. She didn't know how it had happened, she just knew that Quinn was her knight in shining armor, the man she had been waiting for all her life.

The realization that she was in love with a mercenary, a man who was a stranger to her, someone whose background and life-style were as different from hers as light from dark, should frighten her. But it didn't. She might have known Quinn for only a few days, but in her heart she felt as if she'd known him for a lifetime. And in her soul, she sensed that she had known him forever.

Victoria found a grassy spot to sit and wait for

Quinn. The minutes dragged by and with each passing second her willpower eroded bit by bit. If she were more experienced, she would seduce Quinn, but unfortunately she knew absolutely nothing about the art of seduction. Maybe a direct approach would work for her. She could just tell him that she loved him and wanted him. Sure thing, and have him laugh in her face? Guys like Quinn didn't make love, they had sex. So maybe she should offer to have sex with him. *Won't work,* she reminded herself. *He's not into virgins, remember?*

Well, while she figured out some way to entice Quinn, she might as well enjoy the view. Who knows, she thought, it might inspire her. Smothering a silly giggle, she scooted around until she faced the lagoon.

Quinn emerged from the pool, water dripping from his magnificent body—his magnificent *naked* body! Victoria swallowed hard. Every inch was sheer perfection. From his broad shoulders, down his big arms and muscular chest to his narrow waist and hips and his lean, hairy legs. But the part of his anatomy that fascinated her the most was semi-erect and quite impressive.

What would it feel like to have all that wonderful masculine power possess her? She knew one thing for certain—she wanted Quinn to make love to her more than she'd ever wanted anything in her life.

Unashamed, she watched lustfully as he pulled on his damp pants and sat on the bank to slip into his socks and boots. When he rose from the ground, he tossed his damp shirt over his shoulder and headed up the rise. She met him halfway, her heart racing wildly.

Quinn gazed into Victoria's eyes and knew that she had watched him in the lagoon. She had the look of an aroused woman. *Don't give in to your baser instincts,* reason warned him. *You've got nothing to give this woman beyond a brief affair and she's going to want more. She'll want all of you, for the rest of your life. She's a rich man's daughter and you're nothing more than a hired gun, a bodyguard paid for his services. She's a lady and you're a bum. You're a jaded mercenary and she's a virgin.*

"Victoria?" *Don't touch her!*

"I've been waiting for you." *All my life!* she wanted to say.

"I'm here now." *Tell her that it isn't going to happen, now or ever. You're not the man for her and you know it.*

"I'm glad." *Please make love to me.*

She smiled and that smile was his undoing. He grabbed her. She cried a gasping sigh. Was she really ready for this? Was she prepared to mate with a man capable of breaking her in two with his bare hands? She knew the kind of life he'd led, understood his deadly expertise had taken him into situations she could only imagine. He was hard, rough, brutal and often crude. Would such a man as that be a gentle first lover?

"You need it bad, don't you, honey?"

"Please, Quinn. Please." She wasn't sure whether

she was begging him to make love to her or begging him to save her from her own wanton desires.

His mouth consumed hers with savage intensity as he captured her body in his powerful arms. She trembled, every nerve within her screaming. She gave herself over completely to him when he swept her up into his arms and carried her down the rise and over to a secluded coppice embowered with young palm trees. After standing her on her feet, he unbuttoned her shirt and then spread it apart to reveal her breasts.

"Tell me what to do." She lifted her hands pleadingly.

"Let me do it all this time. Just enjoy and learn." Edged with desire, his deep voice dropped an octave to a sandpaper-rough baritone.

She nodded. Her lips parted on a sigh when he flicked his fingertips across her nipples.

"You have beautiful breasts." He lifted both, weighing them in the palms of his hands, while his thumbs raked over the peaks.

She wriggled as tremors shot from her breasts to her feminine core. "Oh, Quinn." Tossing back her head, she exposed her neck to his marauding lips.

While his mouth tasted and tempted, he tugged her pants off, leaving her in nothing but a pair of thin cotton panties. He eased her down to the soft grass, spreading her out before him. Lifting her hands, he laid them on his chest. He hovered over her, bracing himself on one elbow as he guided her trembling hands.

"You wanted to touch me, didn't you?"

"Yes," she replied.

He released her hands, allowing her to chart her own course. She caressed him, shyly, hesitantly at first and then, emboldened by his tortured groans, she explored more fully. When she reached the waistband of his pants, she stilled her movements. He clasped her hand and laid it over his arousal.

"Feel how much I want you."

"You must know that I want you, too. So much."

Lowering his head, he kissed her belly, then nudged her panties lower and lower until they rested below her hips. He rose above her, slipped his arm under her and turned her on her side. She allowed him to mold and shape her as if she were an inanimate doll.

As he dipped his hand into her panties, she writhed against the sensation. "I'm going to take care of you, honey. Just let it happen."

He slipped her panties down and off, then tossed them aside. He kissed the fiery red curls at the apex of her thighs. She lifted her hips, seeking pleasure. While he caressed her naked buttock with one hand, he cupped the back of her head in the other and brought her mouth to his for a slow, seductive kiss that went on and on and on.

During that never-ending kiss, he glided his hand between her legs and inserted a couple of fingers inside her moist folds. He fondled her tenderly, bringing her along gradually, until she rode his hand, seeking fulfillment. When he increased the strokes, he deepened the kiss, his tongue and fingers working in unison to increase her pleasure.

Dripping with passion, she swelled around his hand. He withdrew his mouth from her lips and sought her breast. The moment he sucked on one nipple, he pressed harder and faster with his fingertips. In an explosion of pure sensation, Victoria shattered into a thousand shards of pleasure.

She cried out as tremors racked her body. Lifting her arms, she reached for Quinn, trying to bring him inside her. But he resisted her urging. When she gazed up at him, her eyes filled with gratitude and puzzlement, he hastily unzipped his pants and guided her hand inside to his straining sex.

"Quinn?"

"It's better for you this way, honey."

He tutored her willing hand, showing her how to stroke him, where to apply pressure and just how much. As she gave him an erotic massage, he whispered explicit words and phrases into her ear, telling her all the things he wanted to do to her. Then when he reached the limit, he instructed her on the speed of her caresses. She obeyed his every command until he moaned deep in his throat and jetted his release.

When the aftershocks of his climax tapered off, he pulled her into his arms and kissed her thoroughly. She curled up against him, her head resting on his chest.

"Why didn't you—"

He pressed his index finger across her lips. "We

both needed release, but this way, you still have your virginity intact.''

"But I wanted you to be the first.'' She kissed his damp chest.

Threading his fingers through her hair, he cradled the back of her head in his hand. "You want the man you'll spend the rest of your life with to be the first. And I'm not that man, princess.''

"Oh.'' She curled closer, wanting this moment to last, knowing that if Quinn had his way, what they had just shared would be all they'd ever have together.

He slapped her on the behind. "I wish we could stay here longer, but we'd better head out soon, if we intend to make it to Gurabo before nightfall.''

"You're right, as always.'' If today was all she would ever have of him, she regretted that it had to end so soon. But there was much more at stake here than her heart. If they didn't make it to Gurabo, they could both lose their lives. "I'll be ready to leave in a few minutes.''

They didn't find a boat in the first village, which was half a mile inland, so they traveled downstream, hoping for better luck in the second village. As thieves in the night, they crept up on the outskirts and watched the residents as they went about their daily chores. Apparently the war hadn't touched them here on the banks of the Rio Gurabo.

Quinn led Victoria past the village and back toward the river, which, only a few yards away, made a sharp turn in its journey to the ocean. She almost cried out when she saw first the fishing nets and then the row of three small wooden boats. Quinn held up a hand to silence her, then quickly inspected the area.

"There's no one around," he said. "If we hurry, we might get away before anybody shows up."

Scurrying as if chased by devils, they worked together. Quinn handed his rifle to Victoria, tossed the backpack into the first boat, then eased the boat off the bank and into the river. Victoria waded in, carrying the M-16. Once the boat had cleared the shoreline, Victoria laid the rifle inside and crawled aboard. Quinn guided the tiny craft farther out into the Rio Gurabo, then climbed in beside Victoria.

"So far, so good," he said.

He winked at her. She winked back at him.

He lifted the oars, dipped them into the water and steered the boat downstream. "Help me keep a lookout for any movement along the banks. If necessary, I'll expect you to take over rowing. Do you understand?"

"Yes. You're a better marksman than I am and familiar with the M-16, so if there's any shooting to do, you'll be the one to do it."

"Smart girl."

"I'm a fast learner."

He grinned at the innuendo, his body acknowledging the truth to her statement. Virgin or no virgin, he'd wager every dime her daddy was paying him that she would be the hottest thing he'd ever bedded.

But he'd never know, Quinn reminded himself. He was going to return her to Ryan Fortune, still the same sweet innocent she'd always been.

He had to reconcile himself to the fact that what he'd had of her today was all he'd ever get. She had been his for the taking and he'd done the noble thing—for the first time in his life.

"Have you ever been in love?" Victoria asked.

Coming from out of the blue, her question startled him. He glared across the boat at her, but didn't respond.

"Well, have you?" she asked.

"Not really," he replied. "I've had the hots for more than one woman, even got a little possessive a couple of times. But to answer your question, no, I've never been in love and I don't ever intend to be."

"How do you feel about me?"

"How do I... I like you. I think you're beautiful and smart and have a big, generous heart."

"Is that it?"

"What more do you want?" He continued rowing, but admittedly the swift current carried them downstream with little effort on his part but to steer.

"Then I'm just another woman to you?"

Her eyes saddened when she looked at him and he knew what she wanted him to say—something he couldn't tell her. "Look, honey, I don't want to hurt you—"

"Tell me the truth."

The truth? Exactly what was the truth about his feelings for her? He did like her. He admired her greatly. And he wanted her to the point of distraction. She was special to him, in a way no one had ever been, but he could hardly admit it to her.

"The truth is that all women are pretty much the same to me."

"And that includes me?"

Why the hell wouldn't she let it drop? Why was she forcing the issue, prodding him until he was bound to hurt her? "Yeah, princess, that includes you."

Emotion clogged her throat. Tears glistened in her eyes. She willed herself not to cry in front of him. She'd been an idiot to think their interlude earlier this afternoon had meant as much to him as it had to her. He had as much as told her so afterward.

We both needed release, but this way, you'll still have your virginity intact.

Quinn might be a womanizer, but he was a womanizer with honor. He didn't seduce silly, young virgins who threw themselves at him. He had given her pleasure and allowed her to give him release without technically compromising her. How damn noble of him! His conscience was clear. He'd left her virginity intact for some other man.

Their conversation came to an abrupt halt and neither spoke for many miles in their journey. Finally, Victoria broke the silence.

"I can row for a while if you'd like," she said,

"Thanks for the offer, but I'm fine. You're doing enough by keeping watch."

By late afternoon Victoria's stomach growled. She wished she'd eaten something when they'd stopped for their baths. But she hadn't been hungry for food then, only for Quinn.

"There are some oranges in the backpack," Quinn told her.

She rubbed her belly. "I am starving. Thanks."

Just as she reached for the backpack, Quinn stiffened his spine and stopped rowing. With her hand hovering over the knapsack, she gazed over at Quinn.

"What's wrong?"

"Listen," he said. "Do you hear that?"

She sat quietly, then heard what he did. "Sounds like a—oh, God, Quinn, it sounds like a waterfall."

"If it is and it's a steep drop, then that means we won't be going any farther in this boat."

"What are we going to do?"

"We're docking the boat on shore first," he said. "Then we'll make our way downstream until we reach the falls. If the drop isn't too bad, we'll come back and take the boat. If it is too dangerous to try, then we'll have to travel the rest of the way on foot."

"Oh, great! Back to the jungle."

"No more jungle. We're probably less than twenty miles from Gurabo."

"That close!"

"Yeah, that close," he said. "But remember

twenty miles on foot is a long trek. By boat we could still be there by tonight. If we're forced to stay on land, then we'll have to camp somewhere again tonight.''

''A difference of less than twelve hours shouldn't matter, but it could, couldn't it?''

Quinn rowed the boat toward shore. ''You are a fast learner.''

They had no choice but to leave the boat behind as they headed off in search of the waterfall. Something told Victoria that they'd never see that little boat again.

Her instincts were proven right when they rounded the next bend and came face-to-face with the monster of all waterfalls. She and Quinn exchanged defeated looks. They knew when something was hopeless, and any chance of surviving a trip over those falls was slim to none.

''Looks like we'll be traveling the rest of the way on foot,'' she said, resigned to spending another night on Santo Bonisto. A night of temptation alone with Quinn.

Keeping to the trail along the river, they made good progress for several miles, then the trail disappeared, forcing them to make their way inland in search of a road.

The sun rested low in the western sky. Quinn checked his wristwatch. Nearly seven o'clock. They might make a few more miles before he'd have to find a place for them to camp. If he were alone, he would risk traveling on through the night, but Victoria couldn't stay on her feet that many hours. Besides, you never knew what you might run into in the dark.

In the distance, thunder rumbled. Victoria glanced up at the clear blue sky and thought it odd that it was thundering on such a clear day. Quinn halted, listening to the faraway roar.

He grabbed her arm. "Do you hear that?"

"The thunder?"

"It's not thunder," he said. "It's artillery fire."

"What?"

"I didn't think we'd run into a battle this close to Gurabo. Damn! General Xavier has already made his push toward the capital. No one expected him to get this far so quickly."

"Can't we just go around—"

He closed his hands over her shoulders. His heated stare demanded her complete attention. "Listen. Can't you hear it? The battle is coming closer to us. That means the Nationalists have the rebels on the run and they could very well retreat right into us, no matter how hard we try to avoid them. We have no way of knowing how many rebel troops are in the area. They could have all inland entrances into Gurabo blocked. Trying to go on to the capital city right now would be like signing our death warrants."

She placed her hands on his chest. "What are we going to do?"

"We're going to find ourselves a damn good hiding place and wait it out," he told her. "If President

Juarez's troops have the rebels on the run, they could push them back for miles and maybe clear up the roads."

"Where can we hide? If the rebels are headed this way, how can we escape them?"

"I'm not sure we can," he said. "But we're going to give it our best shot."

"What—what do you mean?"

"The truth is there's a good chance that wherever we hide, we're going to be caught in the middle between the rebels and the Nationalists. But we can't just stay here and let it happen."

"This is bad. I mean, really bad. We could die, couldn't we?"

She realized that while he was trying to be honest with her, he was also trying to soften the blow, to give her hope where possibly there was none.

"Don't give up on me, princess. I've gotten myself through worse than this before and if there's any way to keep you safe, I will."

Victoria wrapped her arms around Quinn's waist and laid her head on his chest. "I know you will."

Capturing her face between his hands, he positioned her for his kiss. Their lips met and mated with frenzied urgency. Then as quickly as he'd claimed her mouth, he released her.

"About three miles back, we passed what I think might have been some small, shallow caves. If we can make it back there, and if the caves are large enough, we can hide in them. It's our best bet."

The rumble of war grew closer and closer. They

couldn't move forward. Their only choice was retreat.

"Let's go find those caves," Victoria said.

"That's my girl!"

Quinn set a grueling pace, but the ever-increasing sounds of battle drove them on, back along the route that had brought them so close to their destination.

Odd thoughts flashed through Victoria's mind as she struggled to keep up with Quinn. Thoughts of living and loving and dying. Occasionally Quinn slowed enough to allow her to catch her breath and in those moments was when she knew, with the utmost certainty, that if she had to die there, she knew of no better way than at Quinn McCoy's side—his good partner to the very end.

Nine

They searched the series of cave openings, trying unsuccessfully to find one large enough for the two of them to enter. Then Quinn discovered an entrance almost overgrown with vines and small shrubs. After crawling inside, they found a low cavern with damp, moss-covered walls near the entryway, which opened up to over seven feet in height and stayed at that level for a good ten or twelve feet within the interior. Farther back, the cave ceiling dropped dramatically to crawl spaces again, through which Quinn saw chambered grottoes of various sizes, apparently leading nowhere.

"Looks like this is as good as it gets," he told her, then dumped his backpack and laid the rifle on the cave floor.

Eerily gloomy and dank, the enclosure felt like a tomb to Victoria. But for now, it was a safe tomb, she reminded herself. "It's awfully dark in here."

"Once the sun sets and we lose what little light that comes in through the entrance, it'll be pitch-black," he told her.

She shivered at the thought of being trapped in the darkness, with no moon or stars overhead.

"Wish we could build a fire for the light and the heat. It's chilly." She rubbed her palms up and down her upper arms.

"That's because these caves lead down to subterranean caverns. I'd say we're below sea level here and that if we could go farther down, we'd reach an underground spring that leads out to the ocean."

"Well, that's always an option, I suppose." She laughed. "We could swim out to the ocean and then back to shore near Gurabo."

"Actually, if we could reach the levels below, it might be worth a shot. But short of blasting our way through, I don't think we can do anything but go out the way we came in."

"Do you mean we really could swim out to sea from an underground stream?"

"It's been done."

The limited illumination created murky shadows and painted the corners of the cavern black. In about an hour, after the sun set, utter darkness would claim the cave. Quinn opened the backpack, then rummaged around inside until his hand encountered a cylinder. He lifted it from beneath the other items. *"Voilà!"* He held up the flashlight.

"You've had a flashlight all along," she accused, knocking him over and crawling on top of him as she reached for the flashlight.

He tumbled her over onto her back before she had a chance to grab the flashlight, then grasped both of her hands in one of his and trapped them above her head. Pointing the beam of light at her face, he waited for her to stop wriggling beneath him.

"You'd better be a good girl, if you want me to share."

"I'll be good." Giggling, she lay perfectly still.

"If you get scared in the night, you can use this—" he released her hands, then gave her the flashlight, curling her fingers around it "—but be careful that you don't point the light toward the cave entrance."

She set the flashlight down on its face, directly at her side, then lifted her arms and draped them around Quinn's neck. "What other secrets are you hiding in that backpack of yours?"

Gazing down into her teasing eyes, Quinn smiled. "Whatever I have is yours, princess. Flashlight, handgun, ammunition, beef jerky, nuts, oranges—"

She placed her hand over his mouth to silence him. "I'm sorry about my rifle. If I'd been paying attention to where I was going, I might not have ended up waist-deep in quicksand and I'd still have the M-1. We're probably going to need it, aren't we?"

Easing her hand from his mouth, he gripped her arm. He stroked his thumb back and forth across the pulse point on the underside of her wrist. "Our situation isn't hopeless."

She heaved a resigned sigh. "But our chances aren't good, are they?"

He considered lying to her, but dismissed the idea.

Victoria deserved to know the truth. "No, honey, our chances aren't good."

"Then right now—the next few hours—could be the rest of our lives."

"Yeah. Maybe. Anything can happen, but the odds are definitely against us. We can't stay holed up in this cave for long. Sooner or later, we're going to have to emerge and find out what's waiting for us out there." He inclined his head toward the cave entrance.

"If the rebels are waiting for us, please, don't let them take me. Don't let them—"

Quinn lifted her into his arms, then raised her up with him until she was sitting in his lap. After draping her in his embrace, he feathered kisses along her right temple and cheek.

"Could be the government forces who find us," he said. "Let's hold on to that thought. Okay?"

"Okay." She snuggled into his body, seeking warmth and comfort. "Quinn?"

"Huh?" Absently he stroked her back as he held her.

"Want to exchange stories about our childhoods or discuss our jobs or—"

"Trying to find something to pass the time while we wait it out?" he asked.

"If I don't get my mind off the lousy odds of our leaving Santo Bonisto alive, I think I'll go crazy."

"I was born poor and unwanted in Houston, Texas," he said, just the slightest hint of humor in his voice. "My mother died when I wasn't much more than a baby and my old man was a world-class loser, who pretty much left me to fend for myself. I got in one scrap after another and just barely managed to keep out of juvenile detention before I turned eighteen. I worked two jobs to put myself through college and then I got lucky. I joined the navy and they taught me how to fly an airplane. Then after my stint in the navy—''

She kissed him! His caressing hand on her back stilled. He looked deeply into her eyes and wasn't sure exactly what he saw. Was it pity? Passion? Love? Or a mixture of the three?

''What was the kiss for?'' he asked. ''I don't want you to feel sorry for me. I've made out all right, despite my humble beginnings.''

''I don't feel sorry for you,'' she told him. ''The kiss was to thank you.''

''Thank me for what?''

''For being you.''

He stared at her quizzically. ''You're confusing me.''

''You know how scared I am…actually I'm terrified. So to try to get my mind off my fears, you started relating your life story. My bet is that you don't usually like to talk about yourself.'' She kissed him again—a soft, quick brush of her lips against his. ''Did anyone ever tell you how wonderful you are?''

His mouth curved into a smile. ''A few women have told me, but only after I'd made love to them.''

She socked him playfully in the stomach.

"You're still doing it—aren't you?—joking around so I won't think about our predicament."

"I wasn't joking about how grateful those women were after I—"

She kissed him a third time, but didn't end the kiss quickly. Instead she used her tongue to tease his lips. When he moaned, she slipped her tongue inside and explored.

Quinn responded, damning himself the moment he allowed his instincts to take charge. If he had pushed her away that very moment, he might have saved himself. But how could a man think straight when his arms were filled with a woman he badly wanted?

When he reached between them and cupped her breast, she broke the kiss, gulped in air and then said, "I want to be one of those women who tells you how wonderful you are after you've made love to her."

"Ah, honey, you don't play fair." He released her breast, then ran his hand down her rib cage and to her slender waist. "There's nothing I want more than to make love to you, but—"

"No buts," she interrupted. "Not now. Whatever reasons you had for not becoming my lover, aren't important anymore, are they? There's every chance that we may not be alive this time tomorrow."

He wanted to contradict her, to promise her that he wouldn't let anything bad happen to her. But he refused to lie to her—now or ever. Gripping her waist, he pulled her up against him. "Are you sure about this?'' His gaze caught and locked with hers. ''You want me to make love to you?''

She saw the hunger in his eyes. He wanted her as much as she wanted him, but still he was giving her a chance to change her mind. Deep down inside the bad boy mercenary beat the heart of a gentleman.

''I'm sure that I don't want to die a virgin,'' she told him. ''I'm sure that under any circumstances I'd want you to be my first lover, but especially now, with things the way they are. And I'm even more sure that I'm very much in love with you.''

Her powerful declaration knocked him off center. He knew she wanted him and understood her desire to experience lovemaking before dying. But he hadn't expected her to say that she loved him. Maybe after they'd had sex, but not before. A lot of women felt the need to validate sex by telling themselves it was love.

''How can you be in love with me? You hardly know me.''

She slid her slender arm around his neck, but didn't break eye contact with him. ''Maybe it was love at first sight. There is such a thing, you know.''

Quinn chuckled. ''I don't buy that explanation. Hate at first sight, maybe. Don't forget that you admitted to me that you didn't like me.''

''You said you didn't like me, either, but that doesn't mean we didn't fall in love at first sight. They say that love and hate are just flip sides of the same coin.''

He eased her arm from around his neck. ''Whoa

there, princess. When did I get included in this falling-in-love deal?''

"Are you saying you don't love me?''

The look in her eyes pierced his gut like a sharp knife. Her expression was part plea and part dare. "I want you," he said.

"And?" she prompted, obviously expecting more.

"Okay. I admit that I've never felt about any woman the way I feel about you." He caressed her cheek. "I've never known anyone like you. You're different. Special." When she continued staring at him, apparently still not satisfied with his explanation, he continued. "I care about you. You've become more than an assignment to me. If giving up the half million your father's paying me would save your life, I'd give it up in a heartbeat."

Seemingly satisfied with his final admission, she smiled sweetly, then rose to her feet. "I'd like for us to make love while I can still at least see your silhouette." She began unbuttoning her blouse.

Quinn shucked off his boots and socks. There was no reason why he shouldn't take her up on what she was offering. After all, there was every possibility that they weren't going to get out of this alive. While watching Victoria remove her clothes, he divested himself of his shirt, pants, and finally his cotton briefs. By the time he had removed the last stitch, his sex was already erect. Just a couple of minutes thinking about Victoria was all it took to have him primed and ready.

They stood facing each other, their naked bodies outlined by the fading twilight outside the cave.

"I want to look at you. And touch you," she said. "All of you."

Quinn leaned down and pulled a thin blanket from his backpack, spread it on the cavern floor and held out his hand to her. She accepted his hand, her fingers trembling at his touch. He led her down on her knees, then stretched out in front of her like a sacrificial offering.

"Look and touch to your heart's content," he said, then when he saw the way she looked at him, he corrected himself. "But don't torture me for too long. I've got some exploring I want to do, too."

As a child who'd been let loose in a toy store, she lowered her fingertips to his chest and grazed them over the powerful muscles. Then she moved downward across his washboard-lean belly. Placing one hand on each of his hips, she glided her open palms over and under the taut flesh, the well-conditioned muscles of his butt. Then she moved her hands around to slide over the silky hair covering his thighs.

He groaned deep in his throat. She ran her gaze from his tightly clenched jaw, down to his balled fists and then halted at his thrusting sex. Fascinated by him, she straddled him, bracing herself on her knees.

"Go ahead and touch me, honey," Quinn said, his voice strained with control.

"Yes." She reached out. "I want to touch you there."

She encircled him. He groaned again as his sex throbbed beneath her fingers. With gentle movements, she pumped his shaft, using the motions he had taught her earlier.

He grabbed her hand to stop her. "I can't take much of that, so if you want me to come inside you, then you'd better—"

She lay on top of him, pressing her breasts against his chest and rubbing her mound against his throbbing arousal. "Is this better?" she asked. "I know I like the way it feels."

"I like the way it feels, too," he said. "But I don't know if I can take much of this, either."

"The first time will hurt, won't it? I mean, I heard the girls in college talk about what their first experience was like and some of them didn't even like it."

He began stroking her buttocks with his big, hard hand. She sighed and melted into him. With his other hand, he lifted her face, then grasped her chin and brought her lips to his.

Breathing into her mouth, he said, "The first time will be uncomfortable for you, but I promise you that you'll like it. And I'd lay money on your loving it the second time and then even more every time after that."

"W-we're going to make love all night?" she asked incredulously.

"Yeah, princess, we're going to make love all night."

"Oh, Quinn. Thank you."

"No, I'm the one who's grateful," he said. "Thank you, Victoria, for giving me the most wonderful gift anyone has ever given me. No one's ever loved me."

From that moment on Quinn dominated their lovemaking with every touch, every caress, every flick of his tongue. But just as he had suspected and never dared hope to discover for himself, Victoria's sexuality quickly reached a white-hot intensity. The more he gave, the more she wanted.

Not one inch of her body was left unexplored. From her ears to her toes. From her shoulders to her knees. From her breasts to her inner feminine folds. He wanted to give her pleasure, to bring her into womanhood with the ecstasy she deserved. Even if he'd never done one good, perfect thing in his entire life, he desperately wanted to do this right.

Suddenly she reversed their roles and began an assault on his body that mimicked his attack on hers. He allowed her free rein, realizing that she enjoyed exploring his body as much as he did hers.

He'd known she'd be like this—all wild and hot and uncontrollable!

When her mouth descended over his belly, her fingers raking a trail downward, Quinn bucked, anticipating her destination with pleasure. Holding him securely, she tasted him hesitantly at first and then stroked him with her tongue. He dug his heels into the blanket and curved his hands into tight fists to keep from grabbing her head.

Within minutes after she initiated the ardent attention to his sex, he thought he would explode. She seemed to be enjoying herself immensely and he knew he was, but he doubted she realized he was on the edge, ready to lose it.

Reluctantly easing himself away from her intimate caresses, he gave her a couple of minutes to catch her breath, then flipped her over and took control once again.

His fingers dipped into her waiting warmth and found her wet and hot and ready. But he wanted her more than ready. He wanted her in the throes of release when he buried himself inside her. The more aroused she was, the less likely she would be to notice his penetration.

He petted her. She lifted her hips, seeking closer contact with his talented fingers. He spread a line of kisses from her waist, across her navel and down into her damp red curls. The moment his mouth closed over her, she cried out. As his tongue pressed and retreated, then rhythmically repeated the intimate dance steps, Victoria melted into a fiery puddle. With each stroke, the fire sparked higher and higher, until her whole body burst into flame.

While she burned with desire, her body wild with pleasure, Quinn rose above her, lifted her hips and silenced her cries of completion by covering her mouth with his. She clung to him as he deepened the kiss and at the same time inserted himself into her wet, pliant sheath. Inch by slow inch, he penetrated her.

When she grew impatient with his gentleness, she took the initiative by whispering in his ear. "Don't hold back. I want all of you."

For a few minutes the discomfort overrode the sheer joy of having him inside her. But despite the distraction, she urged him to continue. Her encouragement destroyed the last vestiges of his control. With each deep lunge of his sex, Victoria's body adjusted to the fullness inside her.

Just as a tingling sensation began building between her legs, Quinn's big body tensed, then he groaned as if he were in pain when release claimed him. He trembled from the force of his climax. Exhausted and sated, he rested on top of her for a few moments. Then he rolled over onto the blanket, pulled her close to his side and possessively laid his hand on her hip.

Quinn woke to utter darkness and the sound of distant artillery fire. While they'd slept, night had descended upon Santo Bonisto and thrown the cave into a thick black fog. Pressing the button on his watch, he checked the time. Ten-thirty. They had slept for hours. He couldn't see Victoria, couldn't even make out the outline of her body, but he felt her curled up against him. He took her in his arms, lifting her so that he could find her mouth in the darkness. The moment he kissed her, she moaned.

"Quinn?"

"Who else?"

She laughed softly. "It's so dark in here. I don't like it. It's almost frightening."

"Then I'd better do something to take your mind off the darkness." He caressed her breasts, then pinched each nipple.

She sighed. "I like that," she said. "Just what else do you have in mind?"

"Something like this," he said as he rolled her over on top of him. "You're a cowgirl, aren't you, born and raised in Texas? You know how to ride a bucking bronc, don't you?"

"I've never ridden a wild stallion like you before." She encircled his shaft, then brought it up and into her body. "But I sure would like to." Sinking over him, she took every inch of him inside her.

She set the pace of their lovemaking, but allowed Quinn to guide her. His hands tutored her lunging hips. His mouth tormented her breasts. And all the while Victoria experienced only pleasure. Their second lovemaking concluded in shattering climaxes, first for her and then for him. When the aftershocks faded from their bodies, she fell asleep on top of him. Later, he rolled her over onto her side and warmed her body with his.

True to his word, Quinn roused her again during the night and then for the final time at daybreak, just as sunlight shot through the cave opening and illuminated the cavern where they slept. They made love with a tortured madness, born of the knowledge that death might claim them both before day's end.

Afterward, they dressed, ate an orange apiece and shared the precious water in Quinn's canteen. Then Quinn explained that he would have to leave her for a short period of time. Unless he went outside and checked on the situation, there would be no way to know what was happening.

She clung to him, not wanting him to risk his life, but nodded her head and smiled sadly. "Please, be careful."

He removed a 9 mm Ruger from his backpack and placed it in Victoria's hand. "It has a fifteen-shot magazine, but if you have to use it, make every shot count."

"I'll wait right here until you come back," she said, tears gathering in the corners of her eyes.

"If for any reason I don't come back, you'll have to leave this cave and try to find some government troops."

"You will come back!" Gripping his shirtfront in her hands, she wadded the material tightly.

He kissed her quickly, then jerked free of her tenacious hold and headed out the narrow entry. She waited until she couldn't see him, then crawled toward the entrance to the cave. Searching the surrounding area, she saw no one. Quinn had already disappeared into the woods.

Waiting was slow torture. Her imagination kicked into overdrive, filling her head with a hundred and one death scenarios. She had no idea how long

Quinn had been gone. The minutes seemed like hours and the hours like days.

He should have been back by now, she told herself. Something must have gone wrong. Had he run into trouble?

Sitting hunched over at the cave entrance, she heard the sound of artillery fire in the distance. Another battle. And not far from the cave. Parting the shrubs that hid the entrance, she peered outside, but could see nothing more than the grass and trees.

As the battle raged on, the sounds of gunfire growing closer and closer, Victoria held the Ruger tightly to her chest and prayed that Quinn would return to her unharmed.

The noon sun warmed Victoria's face. The sounds of battle grew faint, then suddenly stopped. What was happening? she wondered. Where was Quinn? If he didn't return soon, she'd go crazy!

The thicket to the left of the cave entrance fluttered. Victoria gripped the Ruger tightly. Then Quinn burst through the bush, the M-16 draped over his bloody shoulder. Staggering as he made his way toward the cave, Quinn clutched his stomach with his hand. Blood oozed through his fingers, coating them a bright red.

After pocketing the Ruger, Victoria lunged through the shrubs that concealed the cave entrance and raced to Quinn's side. She lifted the M-16 from his shoulder, draped it over hers, then placed his arm around her neck.

"Oh, Quinn!" Tears streamed down her face as she led him toward the cave.

"I'm shot up pretty bad, honey," he admitted.

"I'll take care of you." She eased him down and into the four-foot high entryway to the cave. "You're going to be all right."

Halfway through the entrance, Quinn grew noticeably weaker. Without hesitation, Victoria dragged him the rest of the way into the cavern. Once inside, she ripped open his shirt and barely stifled a gasp when she saw his wounds.

Oh, God! Oh, God! Please help me to help Quinn. But what could she do for him, with no operating instruments and no medical supplies? At best, she could try to stop the bleeding. If this man had been anyone other than Quinn, she would have accepted his fate and made him as comfortable as possible while waiting for him to die. But this was Quinn, her Quinn, the man she loved. She wouldn't let him die. She wouldn't!

Quinn lifted his hand to her face and wiped the tears from her cheek. "President Juarez's Nationalist soldiers are pushing the rebels farther and farther back from Gurabo." He coughed several times, then turned his head and spit up blood.

Victoria ripped a piece off the hem of her shirt, then wiped Quinn's mouth. "Don't talk. Don't try to explain. Save your strength."

She hurriedly checked his wounds. The best she could do under the circumstances was stem the bleeding and pray. She tore off the bottom half of her loose shirt and used it as an absorbent pad. Covering the seeping wound, she hovered over him, longing to ease his suffering.

Cupping her chin in the cradle of his hand, he ran his finger across her lips. "I want you to take the rifle and leave. Now."

"What?"

"You can't stay here. The rebels will be looking for places to hide. They're bound to discover these caves. If we did, they will."

"But I won't leave you!"

"You have to. It's your only chance." He grabbed the back of her neck, pulled her down for quick kisses on both cheeks, then shoved her away from him. "Give me the Ruger and that flask of whiskey in the backpack, then you take the backpack, the M-16, the map and the compass and head due east."

"No, Quinn. I won't go!"

"Watch out for rebel soldiers. Don't stop and think about what you're doing. Shoot first and worry about it later."

"I'm not leaving."

"Make your way toward the main road that leads into the capital. I think the Nationalists have complete charge of the roadways now. And the minute you see a government soldier, hand over the rifle and tell him you're a World Health Institute nurse from Palmira and you need to get to the American consulate."

"You aren't listening to me," she yelled. "I told you that I'm not going anywhere without you."

"Don't be a fool, Victoria. There's no reason for you to stay with me. I'm dying and we both damn well know it!"

"I love you, Quinn McCoy," she screamed at him. "Don't you know I'd rather stay here and die with you than leave you here to die alone!"

Ten

Outside the temporary safety of the cave, a maelstrom of combat noise exploded nearby. With each passing minute the sounds of battle drew closer. Victoria had settled several feet inside the entryway, the M-16 balanced on the backpack, to await the inevitable. She occasionally glanced over her shoulder to check on Quinn, who alternated in and out of consciousness. Their only chance of survival was if the government soldiers found them. But even if that happened, what were the odds that Quinn would live long enough for a rescue?

Pushing negative thoughts from her mind, she focused all her attention on the entrance to their hideaway. If rebel soldiers invaded the cave, seeking refuge from the battle, she and she alone stood between them and certain death for Quinn and her.

Time dragged by, each minute punctuated by the bass drumbeat of her heart. Moisture coated her palms. She released the rifle, wiped her hands on her pants and then gripped the M-16 once again. Beads of perspiration broke out on her forehead and upper lip. Sweat trickled down her back and her belly.

Suddenly she heard voices. Loud, panicked voices. Men speaking rapidly in Spanish. They had found the caves! Oh, dear, merciful God! Her breathing became erratic. Her hands trembled. Her stomach knotted painfully.

The voices drew near and she realized that there were only two men speaking. She could handle two random soldiers, couldn't she? It wasn't as if a whole troop was preparing to descend upon her.

The shrubs blocking the entrance quivered. A dark head poked through the brush. Thin shoulders appeared in Victoria's line of vision. She followed the length of shoulders down long, slender arms and on to bony hands that held a rifle.

Blinking the sweat away as it dripped off her forehead and into her eyes, Victoria recognized the cap of a Nationalist solider sitting atop the head that thrust through the protective shrubs at the cave entrance. A pair of black eyes surveyed the interior. Victoria realized that his vision hadn't had time to adjust to the darkness. There was no way he could see that she was a woman—an American woman! He raised his rifle and prepared to fire at what he probably assumed was a rebel soldier holed up inside the cave.

"Don't shoot," she cried out in Spanish. "I'm not a rebel solider. I'm a World Health Institute nurse from Palmira. I'm going to back up into the cave and then you can come inside. If you're really a government soldier, you have nothing to fear from me."

"I am Lieutenant Macario Romero, *señorita,* and if you are who you say you are, you have nothing to fear from me and my men."

Fifteen minutes later, both sides assured of each other's identity, Victoria gave orders to the two soldiers assigned to remove Quinn from the cave. She noticed the young lieutenant's sad expression when he took in Quinn's condition.

"We must get him to Gurabo to the hospital as soon as possible," she said. "If we don't hurry, he could die."

"*Señorita,* it will be a miracle if he lives, but I will give you a Jeep and one of my men to take you to Gurabo."

"Thank you!" Tears she had held inside her for hours threatened to explode. *Not now,* she pleaded silently. *Not yet. Quinn still needs me to be strong.* The tears shimmered in her eyes, but she willed her fear under control.

Victoria sat in the back of the Jeep, Quinn's head nestled in her lap. He had lost consciousness before the soldiers had removed him from the cave and hadn't come to since then. His stomach wounds had begun to bleed again and nothing she did appeared to help him.

The trip into Gurabo along a bumpy roadway seemed endless. Along the roadside, bodies lay scattered, just one of the many signs of battle they encountered. Victoria prayed that she'd never see the horrors of war again. She had been a naive fool to have stayed in Palmira as long as she had. She only hoped for the hundredth time that Ernesto and Dolores hadn't been forced to pay a high price for her stupidity.

The capital city hummed with military life. The hospital was filled to capacity and Victoria was told there were no surgeons available to operate on Quinn immediately. She demanded the soldier who had driven her to Gurabo wait with Quinn while she asked to make a telephone call.

The American ambassador seemed overjoyed to hear from her. "Ms. Fortune, I've been on the phone with your father this morning. He's greatly concerned about you. He'll be—"

"I need you to use whatever influence you have to get Mr. McCoy, the man who rescued me, into surgery as soon as possible. Pull strings. Make threats. Offer bribes. I don't care what you have to do, just do it!"

"Yes, ma'am. Just leave it to me. I'll see that Mr. McCoy receives immediate attention."

A week later Quinn had recovered enough to travel. Victoria had called ahead and made all the preparations for Quinn to recuperate at the Double Crown Ranch. Her father had seemed a bit surprised that she wanted to personally nurse her rescuer back to health.

"You don't understand, Daddy. Quinn saved my life more than once. I wouldn't be coming home to you, if it weren't for him."

"I do understand," Ryan had said. "It's just I'd

like for you to spend your time getting reacquainted with your family, especially now. We need each other more than we ever have. I can hire the best nurses available to take care of Mr. McCoy.''

''I know you hire only the best. After all, that's what you did when you hired Quinn.'' Victoria hesitated, fearing her father's reaction if she admitted the entire truth. ''Daddy, Quinn's a very special man.''

''I don't think I like the sound of this.''

''You're going to think the world of him when you get to know him.''

''Victoria, the man is a mercenary!''

''I know that! But then, somebody has to do all the dirty work in the world, so the rest of us can keep our hands nice and clean.''

''You're in love with the man. God help you, you are, aren't you?''

''I'm afraid so,'' she admitted. ''And there's nothing that you or he or anyone can do about it. I'm head over heels, madly, wildly, passionately in love.''

When her father didn't respond, she said, ''You know how that feels, don't you?''

''Yeah, baby girl, I know exactly how that feels.''

Victoria had informed Quinn that he had been ensconced not only in the same wing of the house where her bedroom was located, but actually in the connecting room that had once belonged to her twin sister Vanessa. Although he'd seen, upon their arrival, what he assumed was most of the immediate Fortune family—including Vanessa—he hadn't actually met any of them. Victoria had instructed the ranch hands, who had assisted him out of the limousine, to carry Mr. McCoy upstairs.

There in front of her family, she had bent, kissed him on the mouth and said, "Roy and Ben will get you settled in. You take a nice nap and I'll be on up to check on you after I reassure everyone that I'm really alive and well."

She had taken charge of his life, not once asking him what he wanted to do. If he'd had a choice in the matter he wouldn't have come to the Double Crown to recuperate. He had tried to tell Victoria that he wanted to go home to New Mexico, but she hadn't listened to a word he'd said.

When he had awakened in the Gurabo hospital, she'd been sitting at his bedside. Once the doctors had told him that he'd live, Victoria turned into a whirlwind of activity, planning their return to the United States. She had talked endlessly about taking him home with her, about all the things they would do together once he was fully recovered. She had hugged and kissed him often, which he really hadn't minded at all, but her frequent declarations of love had unnerved him.

Now, here he was on the Double Crown Ranch, lying in her twin sister's bed, with a sizable number of the Fortune clan gathered in the rooms around him. He could just imagine what the big man himself, Ryan Fortune, would say when Victoria told him that she was in love with the mercenary he'd hired to rescue her.

Would her father suspect that his little girl had lost her virginity to the most unworthy man she'd ever known?

He'd been out of his mind to make love to her. Hell, he'd thought she would react this way, that she'd convince herself she was in love with him. If he had to do it over again... What would he have done? Would he have really turned her down when she'd asked him to be her first lover? He struggled with the answer, trying to lie to himself, but the truth was that if he had it to do over again, he'd still make love to her. Every man deserved the right to, at least once, make love to a woman who truly loved him. Even a man like Quinn McCoy.

The hours they had spent together making love in the cave had been unlike anything he'd ever experienced. For as long as he lived, he'd never meet another woman he'd want as much as Victoria.

But just as soon as he possibly could, he was going to have to get out of her life and stay away. No matter how she thought she felt about him, he knew that they had no future together.

"Daddy's been half out of his mind worrying about you," Vanessa said as she pulled Victoria aside. "I kept telling him that you'd be all right, but I have to admit that I was beginning to have my doubts."

"Quinn saved my life on several occasions," Victoria said. "If it weren't for him..." She had never kept secrets from Vanessa. Even as small children they had shared confidences, but even more so when they'd turned to each other for comfort after their mother's death. "I think you should know that I'm in love with him. I want to marry him and spend the rest of my life with him."

Vanessa raised her eyebrows in surprise. "Does Daddy have any idea that the man he hired to rescue you also tried to seduce you?"

"Daddy knows. And Quinn didn't seduce me. I was the one who seduced him. Well, sort of."

"Don't tell me that you actually had sex with him!"

"Lower your voice," Victoria told her sister. "That isn't something I want Daddy to hear. At least not right now."

Before Vanessa could respond, her husband Devin joined them. Slipping his arm around his wife's waist, he pulled her to his side. "Hope I'm not interrupting."

"Not at all," Victoria said. "Besides, I think it's past time I got to know my brother-in-law. I understand you were the FBI agent assigned to investigate my little nephew Bryan's kidnapping and that's how you and my sister met."

"That's right," Vanessa said. "Those were difficult days for all of us. I thought Matthew and Claudia would never survive losing Bryan. And then discovering that little Taylor is actually Matthew's child almost destroyed their marriage."

Victoria glanced across the room to where her brother and his wife stood side by side. "Does Claudia still believe Matthew had an affair?"

"I don't know," Vanessa said. "But if she does, it appears that she's forgiven him or at least they've agreed to put aside their differences until Lily's trial is over. We've all been putting Daddy's problems first these days. Maybe you should wait awhile before you tell him that you plan to marry Quinn McCoy."

"You're going to marry Quinn McCoy?" Devin asked, shock evident in his voice.

"Yes, I am," Victoria said. "Just as soon as he's fully recovered."

"Are you telling us that Quinn McCoy asked you to marry him?" Devin shook his head in disbelief.

"No, he hasn't asked me, but I'm sure it's only a matter of time."

Devin shrugged, the look on his face skeptical.

Just as Victoria started to explain about her relationship with Quinn, Matthew called from across the room.

"Come here, little long-lost sister. I want to propose a toast."

The family gathered together, then raised their glasses as Matthew said, "Here's to the Fortunes of Texas and to the safe return of our Victoria."

Matthew set aside his glass, then reached out and grabbed Victoria in a bear hug. "Don't you ever run off to one of those damn uncivilized places again and have us worried to death about you."

She wrapped her arms around Matthew, realizing her safe return proved to her brother that sometimes even hopeless situations weren't really hopeless. If she could survive a civil war in Santo Bonisto, then there was a chance that Bryan might not be lost to the family forever. "You and Claudia will get Bryan back someday."

He didn't respond, just hugged her for a long time. Finally, when Ryan placed his hand on Matthew's shoulder, he stepped out of his sister's comforting embrace.

"Come say hello to Lily," Ryan said. "I'd very much like for you two to become friends."

There had been a time when Victoria had been certain that she would hate Lily Cassidy as she much as she had despised Sophia Barnes, the woman who had become the second Mrs. Ryan Fortune within a year of their mother's death. The only maternal love and nurturing Vanessa and she received during Sophia's reign as Queen Bee had come from their aunt Mary Ellen. But Victoria already realized that Lily was very different from her former stepmother. She knew her father loved Lily with all his heart, and tonight, after seeing the two of them together, she felt certain that Lily returned his love in equal measure. Before falling in love with Quinn, she probably wouldn't have recognized the look of love in Lily's eyes when she gazed at her father. Victoria suspected it was the exact same way she gazed at Quinn.

Taking her father's hand, she squeezed it reassuringly. "I'd very much like to get to know Lily better. After all, if you love her then I'm sure I'll love her, too."

"You're being very understanding," Ryan said. "Could it be that my little girl has finally grown up?" He led Victoria to Lily, then slipped one arm around each.

"We're very glad that you're home and safe with us," Lily said. "Your father was distraught when Mr. McCoy didn't return with you immediately."

"Quinn did the best he could," Victoria said. "I'm afraid I didn't make things easy for him at first. And when I finally wised up, everything that could go wrong did."

"Life is never as we plan and seldom what we expect." When Lily smiled softly at Ryan, tears misting her eyes, he kissed her forehead and privately whispered something in her ear.

Shortly afterward, Lily excused herself. Cutting short his reunion with his children, Ryan said goodnight. A hush descended over the room.

Her brother Dallas draped his arm over Victoria's shoulder. "Don't feel slighted. The old man's going through a rough time and so is Lily. With her trial date set, it's bothering him more and more that she insisted on her son Cole heading up her defense, after Dad hired the best legal minds in the country."

"Is her son a good lawyer?"

"Lily seems to think so," Dallas's wife Maggie said. "Right now, she's drawing her strength from your father and from her children. I think, considering all the evidence against her, Lily Cassidy is a very brave woman.''

''Well, I hope for Daddy's sake that the authorities find out who really killed Sophia,'' Victoria said. ''It's time our father had some real happiness. He has a right to spend the rest of his life with the woman he loves.''

Victoria sat on the edge of Quinn's bed, her fingers idly stroking his arm. ''It's really wonderful to be home. I'd forgotten how much I enjoy our all being together.''

''So, have you decided to stay in the good old U.S.A. for a while?'' Quinn asked.

''Actually, if my plans work out, I'll probably resign from the World Health Institute and—''

''Hey, that's some turnaround. Why the hundred and eighty degree? Don't tell me that our little experience in the Santo Bonisto jungles changed your mind about saving the world.''

She lifted Quinn's arm, opened his hand and brought his open palm up to her mouth. ''My plans weren't to save the world, just to go where I was needed and do what I could to help. But now I've found one particular person who needs me and I'd like to concentrate all my efforts on taking care of him.'' She licked a circle on his palm.

Quinn snatched his hand away from her. ''If you're talking about me, then that job's about over for you. I'm not going to need anyone to take care of me for much longer.''

"I know you're growing stronger and healing more and more every day." Victoria caressed his cheek, then brushed her lips across his. "But once you're fully recovered, you're still going to need me."

"Am I?" His expression remained somber.

"Of course you are." She kissed him again. "You're going to need me to kiss you." She hugged him gently. "And hug you." She nuzzled his nose. He grinned. "And make you laugh." She tiptoed her fingers under the cover, then cupped his sex. "And you're going to need me for lovemaking."

"I sound like a pretty needy fellow," Quinn said.

"I'm needy, too," Victoria told him. "I need you to get well so we can share another night together like the one we shared in the cave."

Quinn couldn't prevent the erection that formed under Victoria's hand. With her touching him so intimately and reminding him of how it had felt to make love to her, it was all he could do not to beg her to give him relief right this minute.

"See," she said. "You need me now." She whipped the covers to his feet, then crawled into bed beside him.

"Just what do you think you're doing?"

"I'm going to give you what you need." She slipped her hand inside the split in his pajama bottoms.

"Victoria…honey…I'm not so sure that's a good idea."

When she circled his shaft in her hand, he

groaned, then sighed when she caressed the tip with her thumb. "Now, what were you saying?"

"I was saying I think you'd better lock the door."

"I did that when I came in."

While she used her hand to excite Quinn, he reached up inside her soft, cotton sweater and cupped her breast. "I liked it better on the island, when you didn't bother wearing a bra."

"There's a front snap," she said.

He undid the closure, then covered her breast with his hand. His touch sent currents of longing shooting through her body. She nuzzled his neck, then nibbled on his ear.

"This isn't for me tonight, Quinn. This is for you."

"But—"

"Hush, now. You can make it up to me when you're all well. We don't want you bursting any stitches."

She lowered her head. Quinn's hips rose off the bed when her mouth touched him intimately.

"Ah, princess, you don't have to do this."

"But I want to," she told him, then proceeded to show him just how much.

Eleven

Victoria knocked on the bathroom door, then, when invited in, opened it. "Hi, there. Mind if I help you out?"

The adorable little boy nestled in a supportive seat within the huge bathtub turned his head, looked up and smiled. From her position on her knees by the tub, her sister-in-law Claudia ran a small, soft cloth over his chubby arms.

"Why don't you just watch," Claudia suggested. "I'm already soaked to the skin. No use both of us getting wet."

"He's precious," Victoria said.

"Yes, he is." With her gaze riveted to the child, Claudia asked, "Do you think he looks like Matthew?"

"Uh, ah, I don't know. Maybe. But I'm not sure." Victoria was uncertain how to respond to her sister-in-law's question, considering the fact that proof of Taylor's paternity had almost ended her brother's marriage. Had Claudia accepted Matthew's solemn vow that he'd never been unfaithful to her and couldn't explain how the child was biologically his?

"It's all right, you know. I've accepted the fact that Taylor is Matthew's child and although I had my doubts at first, I believe Matthew when he swears he was never unfaithful to me."

"Knowing my brother the way I do, I could never believe that this child was a result of Matthew's infidelity."

"While Matthew and I were apart, we both came to realize that our love for each other is strong and deep and can weather any storm, as long as we trust each other. I should have believed Matthew from the very beginning, but... I think I was still in a state of shock after Bryan's kidnapping."

Claudia lifted Taylor from the bathtub. Victoria handed her the hooded bath towel lying on the vanity. After wrapping the child in the cuddly terry cloth, Claudia sat on the edge of the tub, with the little boy in her lap.

"Don't give up hope that you'll get Bryan back," Victoria said. "Miracles do happen. Just look at me. There was a while there when I didn't think I'd ever see home again."

"I'll never give up hope, but I have to be realistic. We may never know where Bryan is any more than we'll ever know Taylor's true origins."

Victoria held open her arms. "Here, big boy, want to come to Aunt Victoria?"

Taylor went happily into his aunt's arms. Holding him close to her body, Victoria breathed in the fresh scent of a clean baby, something that was on her list of top five wonderful smells. Someday she wanted to have a child. Quinn's child. She smiled at the thought of Quinn's reaction when the day came she could tell him he was going to be a father.

Claudia followed her sister-in-law out of the bathroom. "I don't know if anyone has told you, but we've had some recent assurances that Bryan is still alive."

Victoria laid Taylor in the middle of the bed, then accepted the diaper Claudia presented to her, while Claudia filled Victoria in on the most recent developments. "We received an anonymous note on the one year anniversary of Bryan's kidnapping. It asked for a ransom and designated a drop off location."

"Daddy told me that no one picked up the ransom."

"No," Claudia said sadly. "There was no exchange. But at least the kidnapper enclosed a photograph of Bryan lying next to a recent newspaper, so we know he was still alive on that date."

"Thank God. Knowing that, you have all the more reason to be hopeful."

Both Claudia and Victoria looked toward the door when they heard a knock. Without waiting for an invitation, Vanessa burst into the bedroom.

"I thought you'd be in here, when I didn't find you in your room," Vanessa said to her twin. "You've always been a fool over children."

"Were you looking for me for any special reason?"

"Afraid so. Things are in a turmoil downstairs

and I think we need to present a united front in support of Daddy and Lily.''

"What's happened?'' Claudia asked.

"Maria blessed her mother with a visit this morning. From what I understand that girl is getting more and more irrational every day. Seems she spouted off some nonsense about Daddy not marrying Lily, even if Lily's found innocent.''

"Why would she say such a thing to her mother, when it's clear to everyone how much Daddy loves Lily?'' Victoria asked.

"I, for one, think Maria has some serious mental problems,'' Claudia said. "I feel so sorry for Lily. It's not bad enough that she's being tried for a murder she didn't commit, but she has to deal with Maria's hysteria and wild mood swings.''

Victoria dressed Taylor in the outfit Claudia had laid out for him, then kissed both of his cheeks and handed him over to his substitute mother. "I'll go downstairs with Vanessa and see if we can lighten the mood. We might persuade Lily to take a ride with us or maybe we can talk her into going shopping.''

"I'm afraid a shopping trip is out,'' Vanessa said. "Lily's picture has been plastered across every newspaper in the state. She can't go anywhere without being recognized.''

"How awful!''

"You should see this morning's headlines.'' Vanessa opened the bedroom door. "Come on, I'll tell you the worst of it on the way downstairs. When I left to find you, Dallas and Matthew were trying their best to talk Daddy out of suing half a dozen papers and two television stations.''

"And what was Zane doing?" Victoria followed her sister out into the hallway.

"Zane's on the phone with one of his many bimbos, setting up a date for next weekend." Vanessa shook her head in disgust. "It's high time we found that man a good woman."

"One crusade at a time," Victoria said. "Let's go help the boys save Daddy from a heart attack and then we'll see what we can do to make Lily feel like a part of this family."

"God forgive me for speaking ill of the dead, but Lily's a real improvement over Witch Sophia, isn't she?"

"Yes, she is, so that's why I don't understand how the newspapers can paint her in such a negative light."

"Oh, it's only because of Daddy's money," Vanessa said. "They keep implying that she's just a gold digger...or worse."

The sisters made their way side by side down the stairs, hesitating in the foyer when they heard loud voices coming from Ryan's den. They exchanged looks of sympathetic understanding for their father.

"I'm not giving up on us," Ryan bellowed. "Do you hear me, Lily! Marry me now, before the trial. That should show the whole world how much faith I have in you."

Victoria and Vanessa opened the door to their father's den, but hovered in the doorway, making no move to enter.

Lily lifted her hand to Ryan's cheek. "I love you so, and I know that you love me. But I can't marry you until I've been acquitted. I couldn't bear the thought of chaining you to me if I—"

Ryan gathered Lily into his arms. "I'll never allow you to go to prison. We're going to find out who really killed Sophia. I've already asked Sam Waterman about hiring the best private detective in Texas to back up your defense team."

"I know you're doing all you can, but I must admit that there are times when I wonder why so many obstacles have been put in our path," Lily said. "It's as if fate is conspiring against us to keep us apart."

Vanessa cleared her throat. Lily jumped. Ryan glared toward the open doorway. The moment he recognized the intruders, his harsh expression softened.

"Why don't you two girls go on in to lunch," Ryan said. "And rustle up your brothers and that husband of yours, Vanessa. Lily and I will join you shortly."

"Is there anything we can do to help?" Victoria asked.

"Your being here all in one piece helps me," Ryan said. "By the way, how's your Mr. McCoy doing today? Is he going to be able to join the family for meals, now? He's been holed up in Vanessa's old room for over a week."

"He's much better, Daddy. Thanks for asking. But I'd already planned to take a tray upstairs and share lunch with him. I hope you don't mind. I'm sure Quinn and I can join you for dinner tonight."

"See that you do. We're all together just for the weekend and will have to get back on schedule come Monday morning. I'd like to have all my children around me as much as possible. Besides, we've invited Lily's children to join us tonight, too."

When Victoria carried their lunch tray into the bedroom, she found Quinn fully dressed in shirt, pants and jacket. He stood by the windows with his back to her. When she set the tray on the round table by the windows, he turned to face her.

"I've brought lunch. Steaks. Fries. Corn on the cob. And chocolate cake for dessert."

"We need to talk, honey."

"Let's eat first and talk later."

"No, let's talk first."

She draped her arms around his waist, nuzzled his cheek and pressed her body intimately against his. "Whatever you say, darling. See what an obedient little wife I could be? Don't you think you should start seriously considering proposing to me? After all, I don't think my father's going to approve of his little girl living in sin."

Quinn loosened her arms from around his waist and held them to her sides. "You aren't going to be living in sin."

She smiled at him. "Going to make an honest

woman of me, huh?'' she teased. ''The sooner the better.'' She strained toward him until she was able to kiss him. ''I love you so much.''

Quinn released his hold on her hands, turned on his heels and stomped across the room to the bed. That's when Victoria noticed the suitcase.

''Going somewhere?'' she asked.

''Yeah, I'm going home.''

''When?'' Her heart caught in her throat.

''Today. I've already booked a four o'clock flight.''

''Did you book two seats?'' She could tell from the expression on his face that he'd planned a solo trip.

''There's no easy way to say this…''

''Say what? That you're tired of living the good life here at the Double Crown Ranch? That you're homesick and want to get back to your own house? That as soon as you settle in and regain all your strength, you're going to send for me and—'' tears gathered in her eyes ''—and I'll come running when you call.'' Tears trickled down her cheeks. ''And we'll get married and have lots of babies.'' She gulped in painful sobs. ''And we'll live happily ever after.''

''Don't do this, princess.'' He had to end things today. He couldn't go on letting her delude herself into thinking they had a future. If he hadn't been so damn selfish and given in to his desperate need to be with her for just a little while longer, he'd have insisted on going back to New Mexico the minute they'd returned from Santo Bonisto. But he hadn't been strong enough to cut the cord and set her free. Sorry fool that he was, he had let her tend to him, care for his every need and shower him with her love. And not once had he told her that the arrangement was only temporary.

He hadn't gone so far as to tell her that he loved her, but he hadn't said that he didn't.

She had slept in his arms the past couple of nights and they'd made love despite his healing wounds. Taking her again had been wrong, but dammit all, just how much willpower was a man supposed to have when the sweetest thing on earth gave herself to him with such total abandon?

More than anything, Quinn wanted to take her in his arms and comfort her, to beg her to forgive him. But he didn't dare touch her. If he did, he might not be able to ever let her go. So he just stood there, only a few feet separating them, and watched her cry her heart out because of him.

"I'm no good for you, Victoria. I tried to tell you that. Besides, I'm just not the marrying kind."

"But you love me. I know you do!" She held open her arms, begging him to come to her and make everything all right.

Quinn's jaw clenched tightly.

Do what you have to do, reason told him. *Get this over with and get the hell away from her. You don't belong in this rich, powerful family and you know it. What do you have to offer Victoria? What can you ever give her that she doesn't already have?*

You could never support her in the style in which she's been raised. You've gone and gotten yourself all tangled up with a real Texas princess. The cream of Southwest Society.

And who am I? he asked himself. *Quinn McCoy, a real nobody. The son of a worthless grease monkey from Houston. A mercenary whose hands are stained with other men's blood. A gun for hire who's taken half a million dollars from her father for rescuing her.*

You aren't fit to kiss the ground she walks on.

"Don't stand there and tell me that you don't love me!" Victoria screamed. "I couldn't love you the way I do, if you didn't love me just as much." She took a tentative step toward him, her face wet with tears. "It was love at first sight, remember?" She laughed weakly.

"I don't love you," he said.

She flung herself at him, trying to wrap her arms around him. He knew he couldn't touch her and then do what had to be done.

"Look, honey, it was fun while it lasted, but you can't honestly think that I'd marry you." The pitiful look on her face almost stopped him, but he forged on, being cruel to be kind. "You're not the first naive little virgin I've had and you probably won't be the last." That statement was the biggest lie of all. "What happened between us didn't mean a damn thing to me. I was horny and you were available. Beginning and end of story."

"I—I don't believe you!"

"It's never any good with inexperienced girls," he said. "I prefer making it with women who know what they're doing."

"Quinn, why are you saying these things? I know you don't mean them. Tell me what's wrong and I'll fix it. Whatever you need for me to do, I'll do it."

"Always the girl who wants to solve the world's problems. Well, honey, this is one problem you can't solve. You can't fix things between us because I don't want them fixed."

Quinn picked up his suitcase, turned his back on Victoria and walked out the door.

Quinn nursed the Scotch and water the stewardess had brought him fifteen minutes ago. All the liquor in the world couldn't help him. But regardless, when he got home, he intended to get rip-roaring drunk and stay that way for at least a week. He had just left behind the best thing that had ever happened to him—the only woman he had ever truly loved. But it didn't matter how much he loved her or how much she loved him, he could never marry her. She deserved better than him. She deserved the best man in the world and that sure as hell wasn't Quinn McCoy.

Victoria locked herself in her room and refused to come out. Not even Vanessa could coax her into opening the door. Cuddled in a fetal ball, she lay in the middle of her bed, her eyes dry after hours of crying. Her nose was stuffy. Her head throbbed. And her chest ached.

She had gone over her conversation with Quinn a hundred times, each remembrance widening the bleeding wounds on her heart. She'd never realized that anything other than the death of a loved one could hurt so much. But then, she had never been in love before, had never been ridiculed and rejected by the man she adored, had never had her heart ripped to shreds.

All this time she had been deluding herself, thinking that Quinn loved her the way she loved him. How could she have been so wrong about someone? Why hadn't she realized that, for him, their love affair had been a meaningless pastime?

Hugging herself tightly, she fought to control the tears that threatened to return. *No more crying! Enough of this self-pity!*

Even now she couldn't bring herself to believe all the cruel things Quinn had said to her. Why would he lie to her? Why would he deliberately hurt her? Had he really meant all those horrible things he'd said to her or had he simply wanted a way out of their relationship?

"Either way, he's gone," she said, reinforcing the statement by uttering it aloud. "Quinn doesn't want you and there's nothing you can do to change that fact."

Undoubtedly she wasn't meant to know the kind of love her father and Lily shared, the kind with which Matthew and Claudia had been blessed.

When two people loved each other equally, with the same passion and commitment, nothing and no one could destroy that love. But no matter what her future held and regardless of the fact that he didn't want her, Victoria knew one thing for certain—she would love Quinn McCoy until the day she died.

Ryan and Cole followed Lily into the den. When she motioned for them to sit, they did as she requested.

"What's this private meeting all about?" Cole looked to Ryan for an answer.

Before Ryan could reply, Lily said, "This meeting was my idea, not Ryan's. I've decided that...well, there's something...I should have told both of you before now, but..." Tears glistened in the corners of her eyes.

Ryan jumped up, but when he moved toward her, she held up her hands to fend off his advance. "No, please, sit down. I—I... This is so difficult for me. You see, I've kept this secret for thirty-six years— ever since the night..." She stopped to take a deep breath, then continued as her gaze rested on her son. "Please, remember how much I love you, Cole. I've loved you since the first moment I held you in my arms. Never, for one minute, doubt that."

"What are you trying to tell me?" Cole asked.

"Thirty-six years ago I was very much in love with Ryan," Lily said. "And although I cared deeply for my husband Chester, I've never truly loved anyone except Ryan."

"Lily, honey—" Ryan said.

She shook her head, the movements quick, negative tremors. Emotion lodged in her throat. She swallowed with great difficulty. "Ryan and I had a quarrel, which was my fault. I didn't trust Ryan's love for me and I—"

"Why are you putting us both through reliving those painful old memories?" Ryan asked.

"Because it's necessary," she replied. "Because what I did after that argument changed both of our lives forever and—" her gaze settled sadly on her son "—I'm afraid the truth about that night is going to change your life forever."

"I don't understand what you're trying to tell us," Ryan said.

As her eyes glazed over with memories, Lily continued. "Cameron had been after me for quite a while, but he knew I loved his brother Ryan. He didn't care. He wanted me because he knew I belonged to Ryan. That night, after our argument—" she looked pleadingly at Ryan "—Cameron came to me and told me that your father had found out about us and had persuaded you to agree to break off our relationship and go away to college."

"That wasn't true!"

"I know that now, but then... I believed him and I allowed him to...to seduce me."

"What?" Ryan and Cole asked simultaneously.

"He was kind and comforting and I was a naive little fool." Lily hugged herself, gripping her elbows as she rocked back and forth. "I felt so used and dirty afterward. So ashamed."

Ryan shot off the sofa. With his hands balled into fists, he stalked back and forth across the room.

"I couldn't come to you and tell you that I had betrayed you with your brother, a man who cared nothing for me." Lily wanted to beg Ryan's forgiveness and she would—later—after she had finished her story and freed herself from a secret that had been eating away at her soul for thirty-six years. "I realized that I didn't deserve you."

"I should have known you wouldn't desert me without a reason," Ryan said, then slammed his big hands down on top of his desk. "Damn Cameron's black-hearted soul! But, Lily, honey, why did you marry Chester Cassidy if you still loved me? Why didn't you—"

"I was pregnant," she said calmly.

"Pregnant?" Cole's eyes widened with concerned interest.

"With Cassidy's child?" Ryan asked.

"No, the child I carried had been fathered by Cameron," Lily confessed. "How could I have come to you and told you that I was pregnant with your brother's baby?"

"The child—" Cole stood and faced his mother "—what happened to the child?"

"I think you know the answer to that question," she said. "That child was you, Cole. Cameron Fortune was your biological father."

The silence in the room was deafening. Lily held

her hands together in a prayerlike gesture, waiting for a reaction. Waiting for her son to vent his anger and frustration. Waiting for Ryan to reject her, now that he knew the truth.

But Cole only stood there, seemingly in a state of shock. Ryan looked directly at her, then, with moisture in his eyes, he crossed the room, opened his arms and pulled her into his embrace.

Lily dissolved against him, cleansing sobs racking her body as Ryan comforted her. He kissed her forehead. "It's all right, sweetheart." He kissed her cheeks. "You've told us. The worst is over now." Cupping her face with his hands, he wiped away her tears with his thumbs. "If only you had come to me. But it doesn't matter now. Nothing matters, except that we were always meant to be together."

"Oh, Ryan, how can you be so understanding?"

"Because I love you."

Lily turned in Ryan's arms so that she faced Cole. He stood deadly still, his expression one of stunned disbelief. When she reached out to him, he stared at the hand she offered him, but didn't respond.

"Cole, please—"

"I need—" Cole swallowed hard. "I need some time to let this sink in."

"Yes, I'm sure you do," Lily said. "I'm so very sorry that I've lied to you about this your whole life, it's just that I did what I thought was best for everyone concerned."

Cole nodded his head. "I don't think I should say anything now. Not until I've had time... I don't want to say or do anything I'll regret later.'' Cole walked toward the door.

"Cole!" Lily cried, but Ryan held her, keeping her from running to her son.

"Let him go, honey," Ryan said. "You can't help him. He'll have to work through this on his own."

Through her tears, Lily watched her son leave. Her confession had undermined Cole's foundation and had taken away the memory of the only father he'd ever known. Had it also destroyed the love and respect he had always felt for his mother?

Twelve

Victoria sat alone in her office at the clinic, thankfully tired after a full day's work. Keeping busy had become her number one priority. The busier she stayed, the less time she had to think about Quinn McCoy. He had left the Double Crown Ranch more than six weeks ago and she hadn't heard a word from him since. Not that she had expected to hear from him. But in her heart of hearts, she had hoped. Even now, she still found it difficult to believe that Quinn didn't love her.

The first week had been the most difficult. Restless at night, she had slept very little and her appetite had faded until she could barely force food down her throat. Everyone in the family had tried to either cheer her or console her, but not until her cousin Holden's wife, Lucinda, had offered her a proposition she couldn't refuse, had Victoria managed to overcome her depression.

Working at the clinic for underprivileged women and children that her cousin Holden Fortune and his wife Lucinda had founded gave Victoria an opportunity to do the one thing that made her feel whole—helping those who needed her. In the month since she had begun working alongside Lucinda, the two had become fast friends and she understood why Holden loved his wife so very much. Victoria often felt ashamed that she envied the couple their happy life together. She truly wanted what they had. A love to last a lifetime. And a child.

Victoria laid her hand over her flat belly. Even if there was no chance for her and Quinn to live happily ever after, she might still have his child. Missing her period and experiencing bouts of queasiness had prompted her to take a home pregnancy test. When the results showed a positive sign, her first reaction had been to call Quinn. But a couple of seconds later, reality had set in and she'd realized that she couldn't just pick up the phone and call him. First of all, she hadn't been one hundred percent sure of the test results. And second, being pregnant wouldn't change anything between Quinn and her.

Did she want to be pregnant? she asked herself. Was she prepared for life as a single mother? Yes, of course, she was. It wasn't as if she were some penniless teenager. She was an adult with all the money in the world at her disposal. Her child—if there was a child—would want for nothing. Nothing except a father!

But she could give the baby a father, couldn't she? Sooner or later there were bound to be other men in her life, men who would love her and her child. It was just a matter of time until…

Who was she kidding? A hundred men could profess their undying love for her and still the only man she'd want was Quinn McCoy. Damn him! Damn him for letting her fall hopelessly in love with him when he knew all along that he didn't return her feelings.

Victoria snapped around when she heard a knock on the door. "Yes?"

Lucinda opened the door, then peeped and smiled. "I've got the test results."

"Please, come in." Victoria stood, rounded her desk and waited for Lucinda to enter.

After closing the door behind her, Lucinda said, "You're pregnant."

Victoria let out the breath she'd been holding. "Oh."

"You aren't really surprised, are you?"

"No, not really. But with your confirmation, I'll have to make some decisions now."

"Is one of those decisions about whether or not you should contact the father?" Lucinda asked.

"Before he left, he made it perfectly clear that he doesn't want to be a part of my life, now or ever."

"Even so, don't you think he has a right to know that you're carrying his baby?"

"If I tell him and he offers to do the *honorable thing,* I'm not sure I could marry him, not even for the baby's sake. I don't want to trap Quinn into marriage. I love him too much to burden him with a wife and child he doesn't want. If he marries me, I want it to be because he loves me and for no other reason."

"Sometimes marriages that don't begin with love

work out perfectly, when the couple falls in love afterward." Lucinda smiled shyly. "That's what happened with Holden and me."

"You two are so lucky that things turned out the way they did."

"Things could turn out right for you, too, if you'll swallow your pride and call your baby's father."

Sam Waterman studied his employer, noting that Ryan's mind didn't seem focused on their conversation about hiring Annie Jones, the best damn private detective in the state, to back up Lily's defense team. Sam could tell that something else was bothering Ryan.

"Is there another problem I could help you with?" Sam asked.

"What?"

"You seem to be worried about more than Lily's trial."

"Oh, yeah. Well, to be honest, I'm concerned about Victoria," Ryan said.

"I thought she was doing fine now that she's working again."

"She goes through the motions, but the girl hasn't been herself since Quinn McCoy left the Double Crown." Ryan looked directly at Sam. "Do you have any idea what happened between Victoria and McCoy to make him run?"

"I've got a pretty good idea." Sam's mouth quivered in an almost smile. "Tell me something, Ryan, would you like for me to devise a plan to put Victoria and Quinn together and then allow nature to take its course?''

Ryan studied his chief of security for several minutes, then grunted. ''What I want more than anything is my daughter's happiness.''

''Even if being with Quinn McCoy is what it'll take to make her happy?''

''If she can't be happy without that man, then dammit, yes,'' Ryan said begrudgingly.

Two hours later, after devising what he considered a full-proof plan to reunite Victoria and Quinn, Sam Waterman knocked on Victoria's door.

''Sam!'' she gasped, obviously surprised to see him.

''May I come in?''

''Certainly.'' She ushered him inside, then closed the door. ''Is there a problem? Something to do with Lily's trial or—''

''It's Quinn,'' Sam said, his face extremely somber.

''Quinn? What's wrong with Quinn?''

''I'm afraid the injuries he received while rescuing you from Santo Bonisto are still giving him problems.''

''Is he in the hospital?'' Victoria asked, concern evident in her voice.

''Well, now, you see, that's the problem. Being the stubborn cuss that he is, Quinn's refusing to go to the hospital.''

"But if his wounds haven't healed properly, why—"

"He won't listen to me or to anybody else," Sam said. "I was hoping…well, I figured if you still care anything about him, then maybe you'd fly up to New Mexico and talk some sense into him." When Sam noticed the uncertainty in her eyes, he played his trump card. "He desperately needs you, Victoria."

After assuring her father and Lily that she would be only a phone call away if they needed her, Victoria took the first flight out of San Antonio the next morning. After arriving in Santa Fe, she rented a car and, following Sam's directions, drove out to Quinn's secluded mountainside home.

She parked the rental car in the driveway, then stepped back and inspected the sprawling wood, stone and glass structure. The place suited Quinn— rugged, masculine and solid.

Nervously, with her heart pounding a staccato beat, Victoria walked up the steps, onto the front porch and then lifted the door knocker. After several raps, she waited. No response. She knocked again, more forcefully. Still no one came to the door.

Dear God, had Quinn passed out? Was he lying on the floor unconscious? How could she find a way to get inside the house to help him? If necessary, she'd just have to break a window.

While considering the possibility of hurling rocks through a windowpane, Victoria heard a sound from the back of the house. She listened carefully and realized someone was chopping wood. Then Quinn wasn't alone. Thank goodness. Someone was here taking care of him.

She hurried around the side of the house, eager to meet Quinn's caretaker. But she stopped dead still in the backyard when she recognized the bare-chested man with the ax in his hand. Quinn McCoy, his lean belly marred by thick red scars, wielded the heavy tool with apparent ease.

Sam had lied to her! There wasn't a damn thing wrong with Quinn! Why had Sam done this to her?

As if sensing that someone was watching him, Quinn propped the ax head on the ground, then turned around slowly.

"Victoria!"

He gazed at her as if she were the most welcome sight in the world. He was glad to see her, she thought. And in that one moment before he emotionally withdrew from her, Victoria saw plainly what Quinn was really feeling. A man didn't look at a woman that way, if she meant nothing to him.

"What the hell are you doing here?" Quinn asked, his voice as harsh as his question was rude.

"Sam Waterman told me that you needed me," she replied.

"He did, did he? Humph!" Quinn lifted the ax. "Well, you can see for yourself that I don't need you." He pelted the ax into the wood, chopping the log in two.

Oh, no, you don't, Victoria thought. *You can't get*

rid of me that easily. Not now that you've given me a glimpse of the truth. You lied to me when you said that what we'd shared didn't mean a thing to you, that sex with me hadn't been any good because I was so inexperienced. You didn't mean any of those horrible things you said to me that day. So, I'm going to hang around here until I get you to admit that you love me.

"Actually, what I see is a man all alone, a man who needs some company," Victoria said as she took several steps toward him.

"I'm alone by choice," he told her. "And if I want company—female company—then I know where to find it."

"Oh, I see." She repressed the smile that quivered on her lips. "You probably have a little black book filled with the phone numbers of numerous experienced women who are really good in the sack."

Quinn's face flushed. The smile she'd been fighting broke free, curving her lips softly. He kicked at the ground, his movements reminiscent of a bull preparing to charge.

"Look, princess, I think it was damn nice of you to come check on me, all things considered," Quinn said. "But now that you see I'm just fine, there's no reason for you to stay, is there?"

She walked right up to him, a warm smile on her lips, a twinkle in her eyes. "Oh, but that's where you're wrong. There is a reason for me to stay."

"What reason could there possibly be?" When

she moved closer, her body almost touching his, Quinn took a step backward.

"Well, it's like this, Mr. McCoy." She moved in on him, brushing her body lightly against his, her smiled widening when she noted the stricken look on his face. "I've spent six weeks torn between loving you and hating you. I've cried a river of tears and I've gone over every word you said to me a thousand times."

"I didn't mean to hurt you." Quinn gazed into her eyes. "I told you from the beginning that I was the wrong man for you."

"I know you did, and I've taken that into consideration. But I've come to the conclusion that you're wrong."

"What do you mean, I'm wrong?"

"You're wrong about yourself and about me. Actually, you're wrong about us." She lifted her arms up and placed them around his neck. "You're the right man for me. I'm the right woman for you. We're perfect for each other."

"Are you out of your mind?" He pulled her hands from around his neck, then turned his back on her. "Go home, Victoria. Back to where you belong. And leave me the hell alone."

He tramped across the yard toward the back porch. Victoria squared her shoulders, tilted her chin and marched right after him.

"I've decided that I belong here with you, so I'm not going anywhere."

Quinn stopped so abruptly that Victoria skidded

to prevent herself from running into his back. Lightning-fast, he whirled around to face her. His eyes narrowed to slits. The pulse in his neck bulged.

"Just what do I have to say to you to make you leave?" he asked.

"Well, why don't you try telling me that you don't love me," she suggested, then laughed. "But then we'd both know you were lying." Before he had a chance to reply, she said, "Or you could tell me that what we had together was fun while it lasted, but it didn't mean anything to you. But of course, we know that's not true."

He looked at her incredulously, as if seeing the real Victoria Fortune for the first time.

What sort of game was she playing? he wondered. She was acting as if she hadn't believed a word he'd said the day he'd left the Double Crown six weeks ago.

Victoria snapped her fingers. "I've got it. Why don't you tell me that sex is never all that good with inexperienced girls, so it was really lousy with me because I was a virgin?"

"Victoria!" Quinn warned, her name grinding through his clenched teeth.

"And if that doesn't work, just remind me that I wasn't the first virgin you'd deflowered and I probably won't be the last."

He didn't like that broad grin on her face or that devilish sparkle in her eyes. In this kind of mood, Victoria could be dangerous. "All right, so I lied about that one," he admitted reluctantly. "You were the first and will probably be the only, since I don't make a habit of—''

She laid her left hand on his right shoulder, her touch claiming him as surely as if she'd hog-tied him. "No probably to it. Not only won't you ever initiate another virgin, you're not ever going to have sex with any other woman. You're going to be too busy keeping me satisfied to even think about anyone else.''

"This has gone far enough," Quinn said, a nervous edge to his voice. "I think I know what's going on here. If you've got it into your head that I wasn't completely honest with you about…about things, then I'm willing to admit that you could be right.''

Smiling confidently, she laid her right hand on his left shoulder. "Do tell." She patted her foot rhythmically on the ground.

"But I said what I did that day for your own good." He wished she'd stop looking at him that way—as if she were getting ready to pounce on him any minute now. "Marriage between us wouldn't work. Heck, I don't even want to get married. And you'd be crazy to saddle yourself with a bum like me.''

"Would I?" She eased closer and closer to him, until only a hairbreadth separated their bodies.

"I'm the kind of guy who, if I ever did get married, would want to support my own wife and kids. I couldn't handle having to compete with your father's millions. And in the long run, you'd resent having to lower your standard of living.''

She pressed her body against his and laughed softly when he sucked in his breath. "You must have me confused with some other heiress you rescued. I'm the girl who was living in abject poverty in a Third World country, doing without most of life's amenities, when we met. I've never had a closet filled with designer dresses. I've never driven an expensive sports car. And I've been too busy trying to help those less fortunate, trying to right some of this world's wrongs, to have time to be a social butterfly."

Quinn opened his mouth to speak, but Victoria continued. "I know you're not a multi-millionaire like my father, but you're hardly penniless. After all, you do have the five hundred thousand you earned rescuing me. But we should probably put that away for the future, so the children can attend some really good colleges."

"The children?" Quinn gulped.

"And I like the idea that you'd prefer us to get by on our own, without any help from my family." She rubbed herself intimately against him. "And I like the idea of our secluding ourselves away up here in the mountains and building a simple, meaningful life for ourselves and our children, a comfortable distance away from my family."

"You keep talking about children."

She brushed her lips tenderly across his. With trembling hands, he reached out and grabbed her shoulders.

"Are you ready to ask me to marry you?" she inquired.

"What?"

"I said are you ready to—"

"I heard what you said, but I don't understand you."

"I don't think understanding your wife is a requirement for marriage." She kissed him again.

Keeping his hands clasped to her shoulders, he pushed her back, separating their bodies. "I'm going to say this one more time—go home. Leave me alone. I'm not going to marry you. Not now. Not ever. Give it up, honey."

"Okay, if that's the way you want it," she said. "I was hoping you wouldn't be so stubborn, but if you're going to play hard to get, I have no choice but live in sin with you."

When she pulled away from him, he stood there dazed, feeling as if he'd just been sucker-punched. Before he realized what was happening, Victoria hurried past him, opened the back door and flew into his house.

"Oh, I like our kitchen. It's big and roomy, with all new appliances," she said. "Is the rest of the house this nice? I hope our bedroom is, since I'm sure we'll be spending a lot of time in there."

Coming out of shock, Quinn bounded into the kitchen, but didn't catch Victoria until she was half-way down the hallway. He grabbed her arm and spun her around to face him.

"You aren't moving in here with me."

"Of course I am." She patted him affectionately on the chest. "I know you don't have any prior experience in these matters, never having been in love before. But you should know that when people love each other the way we do, they usually live together."

Had Victoria lost her mind? he wondered. Or had he? The woman was like a steamroller, barging in and taking over his life.

"So, that's it?" he asked. "You're moving in and I don't have any say about it?"

She patted him on the chest again. "I brought only one bag, honey. Be a dear and get it out of the car for me. Then you can show me to our bedroom." She slipped a finger between the buttons on his shirt and caressed his chest. "And if you ask me nicely, we'll give the mattress on your bed a real workout before lunch."

She winked wickedly at him. He groaned and rolled his eyes in exasperation.

Okay, he'd humor her, Quinn decided. He'd show her around the house. He'd even fix lunch for her. But then she was leaving, even if he had to carry her to the airport himself and personally see her onto a plane headed back to Texas. No way was she going to move in with him.

A week later Victoria hummed merrily in Quinn's big kitchen as she prepared breakfast for them. She had a hunch that today would be the day. After all, Quinn couldn't take much more. From the very be-

ginning, it had been only a matter of time until he
surrendered. Oh, he had put up a good fight, one
worthy of any true warrior, but in the end she would
defeat him because this was one battle he really
didn't want to win.

He had tried every way under the sun to get rid
of her, but she'd dug in her heels. She had crawled
into bed with him every night, and the first four
nights he'd gotten up and moved to another bedroom. But after she'd dared him to sleep beside her,
he had shared a bed with her the past two nights,
just to prove he could resist her. She had taken every
opportunity to try to seduce him. And she'd come
darn close more than once. God, the man had a will
of iron!

But desperate times called for desperate measures.
With each passing day, she upped the ante just a bit.
Last night, she'd played her ace in the hole—she
had slept totally nude. She was certain Quinn hadn't
slept a wink.

The poor guy had been walking around with an
erection for a week and unless she missed her guess,
he was just about ready to explode. And if she knew
Quinn, he would propose to her before they made
love again. Oh, she definitely had him hooked. All
she had to do now was reel him in. After he pro-
fessed his undying love and asked her to marry him,
she'd tell him about their baby. But until then, it
would be her little secret.

"Good morning, darling," she said cheerfully

when, still wearing his bathrobe, he stomped into the kitchen.

His bloodshot eyes glared at her. "You aren't going anywhere, are you? No matter what I say or do, you won't leave."

"Of course I'm not ever going to leave you," she said. "I love you."

"You love me just the way I am, warts and all. White trash childhood, mercenary background, lots of other women before I met you. None of that matters to you, does it?"

"Nope." She took a carton of eggs from the refrigerator. "The only thing that matters to me is that we love each other."

"You honest to God want to spend the rest of your life being my wife, living on what we can earn, not taking anything from your father?"

"All I want in this whole world is you, our children, and to continue finding a way to help other people through my work." One by one she removed six eggs, cracked them on the edge of a large bowl and then dropped yolk and white into a skillet. "Without you, I can never be truly happy."

Quinn pulled her into his arms. She went willingly. "Why should a woman like you want to spend the rest of her life with a guy like me? Tell me, Victoria, how did I get so lucky?"

She draped her arms around his neck and, with a straight face, said, "Because you're really, really good in the sack."

Quinn's jaw dropped. Then he chuckled. "If

that's the case, maybe I should show you just how right you are.''

He swept her up into his arms, carried her down the hall and into his bedroom. After dropping her in the center of the king-size bed, he removed his robe. Victoria gasped with delight when she saw he was completely naked. Hurriedly, she shucked off her robe. When he placed one knee on the mattress, she opened her arms to him.

He started to lunge, then stopped and said, ''If you want a big wedding, with the white gown and all the fancy frills, that's fine with me. Let your old man throw you one hell of a send-off. But after that, you'll be my wife and my responsibility. Is that understood?''

She smiled shyly. ''Was that by any chance a proposal of marriage?''

''Huh?'' Realizing that he hadn't actually proposed, Quinn laughed. ''Victoria Fortune, I love you. Will you marry me?''

She crawled to the edge of the bed, her movements mimicking a sleek, feline predator as she moved in for the kill. ''Maybe.''

''Maybe?'' Quinn grabbed her, tossed her onto her back and came down over her. ''Maybe?'' He thrust deeply inside her, filling her completely.

She gasped with pleasure. ''Yes. Yes, I'll marry you!''

''I'd like to torment you the way you've been tormenting me this past week,'' he said, thrusting, retreating and then thrusting again. "But I'm afraid any slow torture will have to wait for another time."

They made love with a savage wildness born of their passion. Taking and giving. Tossing and turning. Exchanging the dominant position several times in their mating fury. And then just as Victoria felt herself spiraling into an earth-shattering release, Quinn groaned, then increased the pace to achieve fulfillment and give them simultaneous orgasms. The aftershocks trembled through their bodies as they lay with their arms and legs entangled and their lips exchanging kisses of happiness and gratitude.

Quinn sheltered Victoria in the curve of his big body, then reached down and pulled the top sheet up and over them. He leaned down and kissed her forehead.

"Quinn?"

"Huh?"

"I want us to get married as soon as possible."

"I'm ready whenever you are, princess, but we could wait until after Lily's trial, if you want to. That way, your family would have time to plan something really special."

"I don't want to wait." She curled her fingers in his chest hair. "Besides, I've never had my heart set on a big, fancy wedding. I'd rather we had a small, family wedding. And soon. Maybe in that little country church not far from the Double Crown."

"Whatever you want, honey, but why the rush? You don't have to worry that I'll change my mind."

"No way you're getting out of marrying me," she

told him. "And the sooner the better. I really want to become Mrs. Quinn McCoy before I start showing."

"Before you start doing what?" Quinn shot straight up in bed and stared down at Victoria.

"I'd like for us to get married before it becomes obvious that I'm pregnant."

"You're pregnant?"

"Uh-huh. It probably happened that night in the cave in Santo Bonisto."

Quinn ran his hands over her shoulders, down her slender waist and then let his fingertips hover over her still flat stomach. "My baby! You're going to have my baby?"

Taking his hand in hers, she brought it down to her belly. "In about seven months, you, Quinn McCoy, are going to become a father."

He engulfed her in his embrace. Then he cupped her face as he gazed at her, his eyes filled with love and wonder and indescribable gratitude. "I love you so much." He kissed her, then said, "I'll try my best to be a good husband and a good father."

"I know you will."

"No more mercenary assignments for me. For quite some time now, I've been considering a job offer from Sam. He thinks I'd be an asset to his security firm. And I've also thought about the possibility of starting my own business as a private pilot."

Victoria pulled him back down into the bed. "It's your decision. Whatever you want to do is fine with me. I don't care which job you decide on, just as long as you give up rescuing heiresses.''

Quinn kissed her, branding her as his woman now and forever. ''You're the last one, princess. I promise.''

* * * * * *

Here's a preview of next month's

*Will gorgeous, cunning attorney
Cole Cassidy and fiery private eye
Annie Jones find love when they reunite
to solve the mystery of
Sophia Fortune's murder in*

WEDLOCKED?!

by Pamela Toth

"**You** aren't going to prison," Cole Cassidy promised the woman seated across the table from him. Even though their relationship had recently become strained, Lily was still his mother. "I'll do everything I can to clear you."

Lily abandoned her surveillance of the restaurant's entry long enough to glance at Cole. The pressure of the last few weeks had left shadows beneath her dark eyes, but she was still a beautiful woman.

"You believe that I didn't murder Sophia Fortune, don't you?" she asked, an uncharacteristic quaver in her husky voice. "I swear I'm telling the truth."

Cole leaned forward and squeezed her hand. It was icy cold. "I know you're innocent," he replied. "You don't have to convince me."

"The prisons are full of innocent people." Her fingers shifted restlessly as she waited for the arrival of her fiancé, Ryan Fortune. He was bringing with him the private investigator he'd hired to dig up enough evidence to clear Lily of the murder charge for which she was out on bail.

Cole wanted to reassure his mother, to tell her he

knew she would never lie to him. Yet she had lied—repeatedly—by omission, and that knowledge stood between them like an elephant both were pretending they couldn't see.

Before he could think of something to say about her honesty that wouldn't reek of irony, Lily's attention was diverted. Recognition hummed through the room as her fiancé, the head of the Fortune empire, stopped in the entryway. As soon as he spotted Lily, his weathered face relaxed into a smile. Then, as Cole got to his feet, Ryan leaned down and spoke to the woman at his side.

As the two of them came toward Cole's table, identification and disbelief double-teamed him, driving the air from his chest like a one-two punch to the gut.

Lily glanced up. "Is something wrong?"

Her voice was nearly drowned out by the sudden roaring in Cole's ears. It couldn't be—and yet it was. The riot of brown curls, the heart-shaped face and those wide, kissable lips—the image was seared into his memory like the scar from a red-hot branding iron.

The woman with Ryan was Annie Jones, the same woman Cole had left behind six years before when he'd moved to Denver.

The moment Annie recognized the tall, dark-haired man waiting for Ryan, an icy hand squeezed her heart with painful ferocity. Pride was all that kept her from stopping dead in her tracks.

Ryan must have sensed her hesitation as he led

her to the table. "Lily and her son make a handsome pair, don't they?" he asked. Without waiting for a reply, he leaned over to give the woman with Cole Cassidy a quick kiss on her upturned mouth.

If the man who'd hired Annie had been anyone else in the Lone Star State, no matter how wealthy, powerful or well-connected, she would have ditched the case and walked away. Unfortunately, she owed Ryan Fortune far too much to even consider letting him down. Since quitting wasn't an option, she straightened her spine, curved her mouth into a cool smile and did her best to mask the turmoil scrambling her insides like a butter churn.

"Hello, Cole," she said before Ryan could begin the introductions. "How have you been?" For good measure, Annie extended her hand.

If her calm demeanor surprised him, Annie's former lover gave no sign except a slight narrowing of his piercing blue eyes—eyes that had once burned with an intense yet shallow desire Annie had briefly mistaken for love.

It was a mistake she hadn't made since.

After a pause so slight that she might have imagined it, Cole enfolded her hand in his. She felt his touch all the way to the heart she would have sworn had turned to stone after he'd walked out on her. Before she could even begin to absorb the heat and strength of his grip, he released her. His expression was somber, without even the hint of a smile, and he met her casual greeting with silence.

"You already know each other?" Ryan asked.

His tone made Annie curious and she filed it away for future analysis. Right now she was too busy dealing with a situation she had both dreaded and fantasized about—meeting Cole again. "We haven't seen each other for years," she told Ryan with a bland smile before she shifted her attention to the woman seated at the table.

"You must be Lily. Ryan's told me about you." Although Cole had mentioned his mother frequently during their former association, the two women had never met. Annie had no idea Cole's mother and Ryan's fiancé were one and the same.

Silently Annie congratulated herself on the steadiness of her own voice and hoped that her cheeks, flushed by a sudden searing heat didn't glow like Rudolph's nose. Determined that Cole glimpse not a hint of her inner agitation, she concentrated instead on the older woman studying her with a thoughtful expression.

Lily Cassidy had the dark hair and compelling looks that were a legacy of the Spanish and Apache heritage she shared with her son. No wonder Ryan Fortune had been willing to endure an expensive and very public divorce from the woman Lily now stood accused of murdering. Ryan's intended was still as striking as her son was handsome.

Too bad the last six years had been so kind to Cole, as well. Annie would have taken some small measure of satisfaction in seeing that his hairline had receded, his waist had expanded or the clean line of his jaw had begun to blur. Instead he'd grown more attractive since he had walked away from her without a backward glance.

Had some other woman managed to do what Annie had not—to capture his heart and his name?

SPECIAL EDITION

Stories of love and life, these powerful novels are tales that you can identify with—romances with "something special" added in!

Fall in love with the stories of authors such as **Nora Roberts, Diana Palmer, Ginna Gray** and many more of your special favorites—as well as wonderful new voices!

Special Edition brings you entertainment for the heart!

SSE-GEN

SILHOUETTE® Desire®

Do you want…

Dangerously handsome heroes

Evocative, everlasting love stories

Sizzling and tantalizing sensuality

Incredibly sexy miniseries like MAN OF THE MONTH

Red-hot romance

Enticing entertainment that can't be beat!

You'll find all of this, and much *more* each and every month in **SILHOUETTE DESIRE**. Don't miss these unforgettable love stories by some of romance's hottest authors. Silhouette Desire—where your fantasies will always come true….

DES-GEN

INTIMATE MOMENTS® *Silhouette*®

If you've got the time...
We've got the
INTIMATE MOMENTS

Passion. Suspense. Desire. Drama. Enter a world that's larger than life, where men and women overcome life's greatest odds for the ultimate prize: love. Nonstop excitement is closer than you think...in Silhouette Intimate Moments!

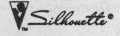

Silhouette®

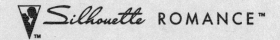